GW00459111

KEEP

KEEP

KAYE BLUE

ROMANIAN MOB CHRONICLES

Keep Copyright © 2015 by Kaye Blue

All rights reserved.

This is a work of fiction. Names, characters, places, businesses, and incidents are products of the author's imagination. Any similarities to real people, locales, businesses, or events are unintentional. This work is intended for mature audiences only. No part of this book may be reproduced in any form or by any electronic or mechanical means, including information storage and retrieval systems, without written permission from the author, except for the use of brief quotations in a book review.

Other Works

Romanian Mob Chronicles

Keep
Fall

Men Who Thrill

The Enforcer
The Assassin
The Soldier
The Con

Welcome to the Family

HER:

I thought the only thing I feared was living another day in the hell my life had become. But when I looked at his hulking, tattooed body, the icy brutality in his eyes, I realized I was wrong.

HIM:

Familie. My clan.

I'd fight for it, kill for it, die for it. It's all that matters to me. But her innocence, only barely hidden by thick layers of makeup, the curves that her tight dress can't hide, calls to me.

So I've decided to keep her.

No matter how deadly the consequences.

1

Vasile

"OFFER MY GUEST A drink, bitch!"

The woman didn't flinch, gave no outward reaction to David Ashmore's harsh tone or insult. Instead, moving with unimaginable speed and grace for one perched on sky-high stilettos, she crossed the large room and stood in front of me, close enough that I could smell the softly floral scent of her perfume.

"May I offer you a drink, sir?"

Her words were low, a barely audible whisper, but her voice didn't tremble. Still, I thought I caught a flash of wariness in her eyes. It was hard to tell through the heavy false eyelashes she wore and the long blond locks that hid most of her face and cascaded down her back to brush her ass.

I continued to regard her, taking in the thick layers of makeup caked on her face, the tight dress that clung to the more than generous curves of her body and exposed more of her ample cleavage than was decent. The dress barely covered her, exposing the fullness of her thighs, her rounded knees, the long expanse of her bare legs.

She was a study in contrasts, painted up and displayed as if she were available for the highest bidder, the ease of her movements and seeming lack of discomfort making it appear as if she didn't mind her body was on display, that Ashmore had talked to her so crudely.

And yet...there was something about her. Maybe it was the healthy glow of her brown skin, the brightness of her brown eyes, both of which told me she hadn't yet fallen to the ravages of drugs or other dangers of the lifestyle. Perhaps it was the distance in her eyes, an innocence, maybe, that told me she wasn't as at ease as she seemed.

Experience had taught me innocence was nearly always a facade, but my gut told me her apparent goodness was real.

Which made no sense.

Good people, innocent people weren't with men like Ashmore, men like me. And if they were, they didn't last too long, not intact anyway. But there she stood, under the clothes and makeup looking every bit the good, normal woman. I tried to meet her eyes again, but she kept them lowered, staring in my direction but not looking at me, and I felt the inexplicable urge to make her, to look into her eyes until I had decided whether she was an innocent or it was all a front.

And on the heels of that urge came the question of why I cared. Whether she was what she appeared, how she'd found herself here, her ultimate fate, none of those things were my concern. But still I wondered, at least for a moment, preoccupied with the conundrum of this woman instead of the business I'd come here to attend to.

The woman moved then, and using those same graceful steps, returned to stand at Ashmore's side. I followed her progress and after a final look, focused on my host, a worm of a man I'd rather kick to death than do business with. But my personal feelings on the matter weren't important. What was best for my clan came first.

Always.

I ran the family now, and was quickly learning that dealing with dregs like Ashmore was more than half the job.

I hated it, would have preferred to be on the streets. There, things were simple and clear. Power was respected, our code held sacred, violations met with swift and brutal retribution. But here, with people like him, I had to pretend to be a businessman, make at least some effort to keep my disdain for Ashmore and those like him to myself, all in the name of peace. It didn't come naturally to me. In fact, I hated it, but if doing so would stave off war, keep the blood of my clan from flowing in the streets, I'd hold my tongue and keep my fists at my sides.

My father had wanted this for me, had dreamed that one day me and my brother would get away from the streets, that I would rise to be leader as he had been. He'd groomed me for it every day of my life, and I would not dishonor his wishes, at least not entirely. He wouldn't have given the woman a second thought, probably wouldn't have noticed her in the first place, but her presence annoyed me, and I needed her gone so I could focus on the matter at hand.

I tilted my head toward the woman and then stared at Ashmore. "Should she be here?" I asked, speaking slowly in broken, heavily accented English.

"She doesn't hear anything, and knows better than to open her mouth if she does. Ain't that right?" he said, looking at the woman. "Can you hear me, bitch?"

The woman didn't move, didn't even blink, just stood on those ridiculous heels like a statue.

"Told you," he replied, turning his eyes back to me. "Heard about your father. He was a great man, and there was a lot of respect between us. But I'm excited about our partnership."

He flashed a wolfish grin at me, his overly white teeth clashing against his tanned, leathery skin. Whether the expression was intended to reassure me or not, it only managed to annoy me more. Respect between him and my father? My father had respected few men and none as foolish as Ashmore.

"Leave," I said, again looking at the woman.

She reacted then, inhaling and then lifting her eyes at me quickly. But she didn't move.

"I told you, it's cool, man," Ashmore said, again flashing a slick smile that only emphasized how sleazy he was.

I met the woman's gaze. "Leave."

Her breasts rose and fell with her rapid breaths, and I could see the calculation in her mind. She regarded me indirectly, not making eye contact, but her gaze taking in every part of me, snagging momentarily on my arms, or more likely, the tattoos that covered every inch of them.

She backed away slowly, tentatively, seeming to have decided to leave but not quite sure how Ashmore would react. And I was again impressed with how she moved on those silly shoes, the sharp *clack* of her heels against the marble floor the only sound in the room.

Ashmore, whose face was now bright red, tilted so he faced her and then barked, "Move your ass, bitch, or do you need some incentive? My guest is busy, no time to fucking wait on you."

The woman heaved a sigh, and to me, it seemed one of relief. Then she turned and practically ran out of the room, moving so fast that I wouldn't have believed it if I hadn't seen it myself. And it made me wonder how unpleasant Ashmore's "incentives" were that they could inspire such stealth. Made me want to give Ashmore a few of my own.

Ashmore looked back toward me, his eyes narrowing briefly before his features softened into that slimy expression that seemed his default.

"It wouldn't have been a problem," he said, seeming to feel compelled to not let the point go.

I stayed silent, not interested in explaining that being here was a concession I'd only given out of respect to his father and mine, but that discussing my business in front of an outsider, a woman no less, would never happen.

"One hundred per week, correct?" I said, turning back to the matter at hand.

He nodded rapidly, head bobbing like one of those dolls. "Same for you as the other clans. Drop it off Friday, and I'll have the clean cash to you by Monday, minus my cut of course."

"Of course," I said and then went silent, waiting. It didn't take long for Ashmore to continue his pitch.

"And that doesn't have to be the only element of our relationship. I can clean as much cash as you need, and if the volume increases, I'd be happy to give you a discount."

He paused, expression expectant like I should be excited about the opportunity to let him get his tentacles further into my affairs. Unlikely. I didn't want to work with him at all, but for peace and for honor, I would.

He nodded again, his brown hair flopping against his forehead with the vehemence of the motion. "Like I said, whatever you need. I like to think of myself as full-service, a lifestyle provider if you will, and I'll go that extra mile for important clients like you. Drugs. Women. Men. Problems you need taken care of. I can handle any of that for you. I know a man of your...status is in the spotlight, but if you need some discreet personal attention, I'm one call away."

He smiled again and the anger that had been simmering in my gut rose into my throat. I wouldn't entrust one cent more of my money than was necessary to keep peace on the streets. And his offer? The very suggestion that there was something he could give me that I couldn't get myself was laughable.

"So whatever you need," he repeated.

Then a devious gleam lit his eye, and he smiled bright.

"Get your ass back in here," he called over his shoulder.

The woman materialized in a split second, which stoked my anger even higher. The purpose of sending her away was so that she wouldn't be privy to our conversation, yet she'd shown up in an instant, proof she'd heard every word. She walked to Ashmore, stood meekly at his side.

"You like her?" he asked, resting his hand on the woman's wide hip and then stroking her lewdly. "She's not much to look at, but she does okay when she's dressed up. Lots of padding, especially on that ass"—he punctuated his words with a slap on said ass—"but she can take a pounding. And her pussy stays tight."

He stood then, and the woman lowered her eyes, but she didn't shrink away or otherwise show the disgust I knew she must have felt. She even remained still when Ashmore roughly grabbed her chin and put his thumb between her full, pillowy lips.

"And she sucks cock better than anyone I've ever had."

He regarded the woman with a glare that was both dismissive and possessive, one even I found somewhat unnerving. But she stayed stock-still. I did too, but only barely. I tried to remind myself I was here for peace, that this woman wasn't mine or one of my clan's, wasn't worth the trouble that interfering would cause.

"Hey, if you want, she can suck you off." Ashmore brightened as if he'd just come up with the most brilliant idea. "Yeah," he said, nodding enthusiastically, "you should let her. She'll swallow every drop. Or you can come on her tits if you want. Not on her face, though."

I stood, somehow managing to move slowly even though the anger in my throat now pounded at my temple, testing my control. The woman looked at me then, her eyes widening ever so slightly when she did, though her body stayed rigid. She was afraid. Of Ashmore, of me probably, and that had the corners of my vision going white with rage.

"Of course," he continued, voice turning coy, "I'd have to watch. Make sure you don't try to take things too far."

As if he could stop me if I wanted to. As if I had to take things from women when they were freely offered. As if I were a victimizing piece of garbage like him.

I stared at him, not moving, though the urge to knock all of the teeth out of his mouth boiled inside me. I couldn't place the source of my rage, had seen women treated worse. But something about her roused my sympathy. Or maybe it wasn't her. Maybe it was the fact that Ashmore had control over anyone, let alone someone who was powerless against him. Someone who couldn't fight back, who didn't have the ability to end him without thought or consequence, something the rage that had my vision clouded almost compelled me to do.

I had no illusions about who I was, where I stood, which was why men like him bothered me so. He was scum. I'd known him for less than twenty minutes and I knew that. He was lower than dirt, and he had no idea. Thought that his ties elevated him. Thought that whatever power he had over defenseless women like her made him something.

In that instant, I decided I was going to disabuse him of that notion, end his life if it came to that.

"Wait a second. I'm treating you like some banger off the corner. But I know you're an important man, a powerful one, and I'd like us to be friends."

The rage that sparked at that suggestion had me taking a step toward him. She flinched, the movement slight but enough that I noticed. Ashmore did not, and instead he stared at me, his eyes gleaming conspiratorially. "I've never offered this, but if you want, you can fuck her."

The woman reacted even more strongly then, inhaling sharply, but just as quickly going placid. It seemed Ashmore still didn't notice, for he watched me, his eyes gleaming even brighter. I exhaled, a sense of purpose beating back the rage, pulled myself to my full height, and then walked to where they stood, towering over him and the woman both. A glance at her showed that she watched me, but I turned my attention to him and stared down at him until he blinked.

"I keep her," I said after a long moment.

Ashmore blinked as if confused, looking worried, slightly panicked, mouth opening and closing, but then he smiled and his face brightened as if a light was coming on inside him.

"Yeah, yeah," he said, voice high-pitched. "You can stay the night. She'll entertain you, won't you, bitch?"

As if I would lay my head in his home.

When I stayed silent, the panic on his face spiked, worry filling his eyes, but still he forged on. "Show him to our guest quarters." Then he lowered his voice, the threat hanging clear. "And don't give him any trouble."

The woman didn't move, and instead stared at me, eyes so wide that even through her false lashes, I could see that her brown orbs were marked with terror, and unbidden, the desire to comfort her, to see that terror fade sparked in my chest.

"Now!" Ashmore yelled.

The woman jumped and then went to move, but I caught her and wrapped my hand around her wrist, the bones feeling delicate in my grip even through her padded flesh. I looked back at Ashmore.

"No. I keep her. For good."

2

Fawn

I FOLLOWED THE MAN, or more accurately, was pulled behind him, fear of toppling off my shoes making me keep pace. He opened the opulent doors of David's home, and the cool breeze against my mostly bare skin made me shiver even harder than the fear that snaked down my spine.

My gaze was centered on the broad expanse of his back, the tight T-shirt that pulled across his shoulders leaving no question of the powerful physique underneath. I kept my eyes there, the unreality of the situation making it impossible for me to look elsewhere, not even as I heard David behind us screaming at the man to stop.

An instant later, I felt the familiar wetness of David's palm around my wrist, and then heard the snap of one of my heels after it got caught between two of the stones that lined the driveway.

"Argh!" I let out a stifled scream as I fell, losing my balance when David's grip on one arm pulled me back even as the man moved inexorably forward.

I braced myself as best I could with no free hands, tried to ready myself for the shock of hitting what I knew from experience were hard stones.

But impact never came.

One second I was falling, and the next I was crushed against a warm chest that felt as solid as the stones beneath my feet. A thick arm around my waist held me, not allowing me to move when I tried to back away. I looked up the strong column of his neck to lips thinned in a cruel scowl and up farther until I met ice-green eyes. The chill I saw there made me back up again, but the arm around my waist still gave no quarter.

And then the man looked away, and I followed his gaze to where it rested on my arm. Without a word, David released me and the loss of his touch pushed me closer to the man. I didn't try to move, had realized that doing so was futile now and instead looked at David's face.

When I saw the rage that contorted his features, everything in me screamed that I should go to him, try to calm him or deal with the consequences. But that wasn't an option. The man's grip was tight, unbreakable, and though it didn't hurt, I had about as much chance of breaking it as I did of predicting what David might do to me if I didn't.

So yet again, I was stuck, torn between these two men, a bystander in my own life, wondering what the outcome would be. I knew what David could do, and though the man was unknown, I didn't doubt that he was formidable. And so I stood, waiting, the ever-stretching moment thick with tension as the men eyed each other.

And then I was moving, the man practically carrying me the rest of the way down the drive. Before I knew it, I was in the passenger side of a luxury car, and before I could even think to jump out, the man had rounded the vehicle, slid behind the steering wheel, and taken off.

Before the gates were completely open, the man drove out and sped down the road. It hit me then that I was being driven away from a house that had been my own personal hell for so long that I never thought I'd get out of it. I'd fantasized about leaving that place so many times that I'd had to force myself to stop. The reality of waking up to David and whatever torture he had planned, the knowledge that I would never be free made the fantasy far more costly than the moments of happiness it gave me.

But those seconds of watching that house of horrors get smaller and smaller and smaller were the greatest gift I'd ever been given.

And when the house was gone completely, the horizon only dark skies and the reddish glow of taillights over asphalt, I turned forward and prepared myself to face what might become my new nightmare.

3

Fawn

I SAT STOCK-STILL AS the car purred down the
road, smoothly guided by the man's huge
hands on the wheel. My fingers had been
locked around the door's handle since he'd
closed it, and as discreetly as I could, I tightened my hold.

"That would be a painful way to die. And I
wouldn't stop to come back for you or tell anyone you were there."

His deep voice sliced through the heavy silence of the car's interior, his words, his gravel-
ly rasp sending shards of ice through my veins.
David had threatened to push me out of the
car before, but I'd known it was all bluster. He
preferred to work in private, wouldn't risk

someone seeing, or leave the possibility I might live. For all the pain he caused, the moment-by-moment suffering that being in his presence caused, I knew David, understood him. But this man...

I knew nothing of him, nothing of what he might do, and that was most terrifying of all. I sat up straighter, not sure why, knowing I had no place to go but needing to do something, anything, to try and tame the fear that had my nerves on edge.

I kept my gaze forward, uncertain how he'd even seen me when he'd seemed so focused on the road. But the how didn't matter. I was on alert now, knew this man didn't miss anything.

It was strange—not being watched, because God knew David did that—but being *seen*. I almost felt invisible around David, tried to keep myself that way especially when I sensed he was in the mood to inflict some of his petty tortures. But this man was aware, paying attention even when he seemed not to be. I'd have to stay on guard.

Silence again reigned, and though the vehicle was large, his presence was oppressive, almost overbearing. Not daring to risk looking at him directly, I peeped at him through the thick fans of my false lashes, certain he knew what I was doing, but unable to stop myself.

I glimpsed his huge hands, which still gripped the steering wheel tight, let my gaze move up bulging arms that were covered with inky-dark tattoos. Another surreptitious glance revealed a harsh face, one set in an expression that could be taken for anger, but that I suspected was just the natural set of his features, hoped so anyway.

And to my surprise and horror, through the fear, there was a stirring of something, my mind conjuring what it might be like to see that face set in some other expression.

I tossed the thought away and averted my eyes, chiding myself for even letting such a thought in before turning my attention back to my predicament. Each revolution of the wheels moved me farther from David, closer to an uncertain future. And as we moved, I cursed him, his pride, his stupidity.

He loved that, parading me around in front of his "clients," his own personal whore to be gawked at, but to never, ever be touched. If I'd been braver, or stupider, I'd have told him what he risked—what he made me risk. David thought himself important, one who wouldn't be crossed, but he hadn't seen, or hadn't cared to see, how they'd looked at me, hadn't seen what I had seen, that threat of brutality I had come to recognize on sight.

Deep down, I'd known it was only a matter of time until this happened, until one of the awful men David dealt with decided to turn the tables on him. My fears had been realized. And I was left to deal with the consequences.

Far too late, I'd realized what David did, what type of men his clients were, and this man was no different. Maybe even worse. David had displayed a level of obsequiousness that was extreme for even him, which told me that this man, physically imposing as he was, had more than size to back him. He had money. Power. Probably both.

And I was trapped with him.

David had done things, things I tried to convince myself I'd one day forget, but he'd never shared me. That he'd offered me to this man meant something significant.

And that this man had taken me without giving David a second look told me something else, told me that despite David's connections, his money, this man felt no hesitation about crossing him, which meant he'd have none about hurting me.

My heart skidded harder, and I wanted to shrink away, curl into a ball and hide.

But there was nowhere to go, so I sat silent, tense, anticipation flooding through me. I sneaked another glance at him, looking for any shift in his completely unreadable features. But there was nothing. So I gripped the door handle tighter and rode with this stranger into the unknown.

4

Fawn

THE MAN STOPPED AND pulled to the side of the road. He got out and stood next to the closed door, his huge form blocking the entire window. I listened to the sound of spinning gravel, heard a car door close, and then a shadowed figure leaned casually against the new vehicle.

They spoke in hushed tones, the language between them familiar, though I couldn't quite place it. There was no urgency in their speech, no particular menace, but my mind filled with all manner of horrors.

Was he selling me? Arranging something with his friends? I knew that people like me, disposable possessions, faced such fates with depressing regularity, and my throat tightened as I considered the possibilities, what I might do to get out of this.

Then he and the other man embraced and he folded his body back into the car and sped off.

I cursed myself, my slowness and my stupidity again leaving me at his mercy. Maybe I could have run away, found a way out. But yet again I'd failed, and yet again I was stuck.

The man drove, not looking at me, not speaking to me, seeming to be unaware of my presence altogether, though I knew that wasn't the case. It had been a very long time since I prayed, so long that I couldn't remember when I last had, but I did so now, my fingers still tight on the door handle as I exalted God, any god, for help, prayed I would make it through this.

When he stopped the car again, he got out and walked around it, his steps all the more terrifying because of his grace. Without a word, he opened the door, stared down at me expectantly, and after a deep breath, I stood and then followed him, hobbling along on my broken heel.

I hadn't known what I expected, was desperate for any hint of where we were, and I glanced around avidly, looking for any clue. But it was too dark for me to tell much about my surroundings, quiet, so still it seemed like he and I were the only souls on the planet.

And so it went. I followed as best I could across what felt like a smooth driveway until he stopped in front of the structure that I presumed was his home. After opening a metal door, he looked inside, silently ordering me to enter. I did and he came in behind me.

And when I heard the door close, the *click* of a lock, I felt the eerie sensation my fate had been sealed.

The man still hadn't spoken, and I watched him as he entered the room, grateful when he flipped on one small light that didn't illuminate the place but at least gave me some sense of where I was. It appeared to be someone's dwelling, though there was nothing personal about it.

I let my eyes touch everything except the huge bed that took up one corner of the space. Silly really, because people like him, dangerous ones, didn't need beds to inflict their damage. But better to not even give him the reminder.

He went through a door, and I heard water turn on.

I stayed still, but when the faucet clicked off, something inside me bounded to action, and I moved back as quickly as my heels would allow, arm outstretched as I groped for the door handle.

"You don't want to do that. It will make a loud noise. And then my men will come and kill you."

His voice was ice cold, the truth of his words clear. And the calm with which he spoke, the absolute certainty I was completely at his mercy, had my heart pounding so hard all other sound was drowned out.

He walked toward me, the black T-shirt that he wore doing more to emphasize his massive chest than it did to cover it.

He reached out a hand. "Take that off," he said, gesturing toward my face.

"Oh..." I said and then trailed off.

"Oh" had been the best I could come up with. Fucking great.

He stuck his hand out again, and I grabbed the wet cloth he held, not wanting to anger him.

I started to wipe away the thick coat of makeup, peeled off the false eyelashes. And despite myself, I felt relief. I hated the makeup, but like the heels, the dress, David required it, and I did what I was told or faced the consequences.

After I wiped my face as thoroughly as I could, I lifted newly lightened eyelids and looked up at him. He stared at me, assessing, his height and heavily muscled body making me feel insubstantial, something I was not accustomed to.

"That too," he said, nodding at the long tendrils of hair that trailed over my breasts and down my back.

"Okay," I said, hoping my voice was calm and placating, not wanting to set him off.

Like the makeup, I had no love for the wig, so I loosened it and then tossed it aside with no qualms, the brush of cool air against my scalp a relief. For a fleeting moment, I wondered how I looked, almost me above the neck, below still purely David's creation.

He stared, glass-shard eyes revealing nothing as he took in every inch of me.

The confusing tumble of emotions that ripped through me left me almost dizzy. His gaze was mysterious but not shy, and I sensed no threat in it at the moment, not that I trusted my evaluations. But still, it felt like he was seeing me. The real me. Something no one had seen for years.

I couldn't help but wonder what he thought.

Then he turned abruptly, and I jumped ever so slightly as if awoken from a dream.

He went to the small dresser, removed a black T-shirt that seemed identical to the one he wore, and walked back over to me, arm extended.

"Wear this."

I looked at the garment, the huge tattooed hand that held it, and then those green eyes, wondering where this was headed. His eyes still revealed nothing, but so far he hadn't harmed me, had been almost gentlemanly. But I knew well how that could change in an instant and hoped my next question wasn't a turning point.

"Is there a bathroom?" I asked timidly as I took the shirt.

He inclined his head to the left, the room where he'd gone before, and I toddled toward it, my heels clicking loud and uneven on the floor. I couldn't tell whether it was concrete or marble in the darkness of the night, but each

24

little *click-clack* seemed louder than the one before it, though all were still drowned out by the pounding of my heart. I felt his eyes on me as I walked, tried to keep steady, not show the fear that coursed through me.

When I went into the bathroom, I took a chance on closing the door. And then I locked it. Standing in complete blackness, my heart pounding, I imagined he'd come rushing in, rip the door open as he raged about me doing something like that without permission, about me keeping secrets, trying to hide things from him. But I heard nothing and as I stood in the darkness for long moments, my heart again slowed.

Groping at the wall, I searched until I found a light switch, lowering my lids when I flicked it on to combat the harsh glow.

Then I set about my task, pulled off the dress and then stepped out of the heels and garter David had insisted I wear. I kept the bra on, though the flimsy material showed my nipples, and did little to support the weight of my breasts, something that was apparent when I pulled the black T-shirt over my head.

It pulled snug over my chest, then bunched at my waist, pulling tight over my hips and thighs. I tried to tell myself that it was no more revealing than that dress, but it was a lie. The man was much taller than me, but my curves shortened the shirt and put what little of my body had been left to the imagination completely out in the open.

I tugged at the hem, trying to make the shirt as long as I could, and then I flicked off the light and exited the bathroom.

It occurred to me then that maybe I should have stayed in the bathroom for as long as I could. But as I'd already proven more times than I could count, I wasn't the brightest bulb in the box.

The floor was cold against my feet, and I padded softly, not sure of my destination but moving anyway.

I didn't see the man, so I looked around the large, nearly empty room, praying he wouldn't jump out at me.

"Water?" he asked.

My gaze flew toward the sound, and I found him leaning against the countertop. His body was still coiled with alertness, but he seemed different, not relaxed but not tense either. But he was still entirely unreadable.

"No, thank you," I managed to choke out.

He nodded and then walked toward the bed. I kept my gaze on his feet, afraid to look anywhere else.

"Come," he said.

I didn't dare disobey him, hoped that maybe if I were good, this wouldn't hurt so much. That maybe he wouldn't beat me.

So heart stuttering, I followed, walked until I reached the edge of that huge bed I had tried to avoid.

He inclined his head again, his intention again clear, and on a deep breath, I climbed in, got as close to the wall as I possibly could and waited.

I shrieked low in my throat when he climbed into the bed next to me, but if he had any reaction, he didn't show it.

He lay down, taking up much of the space, the heat of his body rolling into me, his large form spread out on the bed but still dangerous despite his seemingly relaxed state.

"Cum te cheamă?" he said.

"Uhh..." I started.

"What is your name?" he asked without looking at me.

"Fawn," I said in a soft whisper. "Fawn Michelle."

"*Imi pare bine,* Fawn Michelle. Try not to kill me while I sleep, eh?"

Then he turned off the small lamp next to the bed, and the room was shrouded in darkness.

\\\

Fawn

I JOLTED AWAKE WHEN he moved, and looked around the room disoriented. I hadn't let myself believe last night had been a dream, but I was surprised I'd managed to fall asleep. I had curled in the farthest corner as tight as I could, determined to watch him all night. I'd held out for a while too, the question of why he'd made me change, take off the wig and makeup providing a little puzzle for me to wonder over. But soon, to my surprise, I'd fallen asleep and stayed that way for hours it seemed.

He stood, more intimidating this morning than he had been last night. But the light did give me a chance to see him better, and what I saw made my already dry throat squeeze tighter. His stature was still imposing, the tattoos had the same menace, but his eyes were softer somehow this morning, icy but not threatening, and the raspy shadow of his beard, a few shades darker than his surprisingly soft-looking brown hair had the duel effect of making him more threatening and more human.

And as reckless as it was crazy, I felt a spark of desire low in my belly. It had been so long since I'd felt such a thing, I hadn't thought I ever would again, but the tight thrum that sparked inside me was undeniable.

"W-what's your name?" I asked, my voice breaking from disuse and the dryness of my throat.

Rather than respond, he turned and walked toward the kitchen area of the large room. With efficient, graceful movements, he retrieved a glass, filled it with water and came back to me, glass extended.

"Drink," he said.

Rising up on my knees, I reached for the glass and then caught the almost imperceptibly quick glance he cast at my legs. Belatedly, I remembered that I was clad in a not nearly long enough T-shirt and that my thighs were completely exposed. I froze, torn between the desire to cover myself and the desire not to upset him.

But he did the most unexpected thing—he looked back into my eyes. It was a simple gesture, hardly notable, but it allayed my fears more than anything else could have. He didn't leer at me, hadn't touched me, and that made me want to trust him.

The first drops of cool water against my tongue were refreshing, and I drank eagerly until the water was gone.

"More?" he asked, his voice a deep rumble in his chest.

I shook my head.

"He's your husband?" he asked.

I shook my head again. "N-no."

"Do you want to go back?" he asked.

"No." I spoke emphatically this time, knowing that no matter what, I couldn't go back there.

He stood aside, gestured toward the front door. "You are free to go," he said.

As modestly as I could, I crawled out of the bed and stood, drawing as close to him as I dared. Then I looked toward the door, then back at him, my heart pounding harder than it had before.

He was offering a way out, the thing I had dreamed of, but my feet were rooted to the floor. I looked between him and the door again, sickening dread filling my stomach.

David would take me back. He always found me and took me back. But maybe here...

I met the man's gaze head-on.

"I want to stay."

5

Vasile

I NARROWED MY EYES at her, taking in the stubborn tilt of her chin, the spark of intensity that flashed in her eyes, the first sign of fight I'd seen in her.

"Why?" I asked, assessing her.

"He won't let me go. Not ever."

The resignation and certainty with which she spoke were more tragic than the implication of the words. Bare of makeup, her eyelids not weighted by lashes, she looked younger, prettier, the fresh-faced innocence I'd glimpsed last night on full display now. As were the shadows that haunted her amber-brown eyes. Whatever she faced with Ashmore was worse than being with me, a person she didn't know and one she likely didn't want to. And fuck if for some crazy reason I wanted her to stay.

"I am Vasile Petran. You are welcome here."

A faint smile curved her lips and the shadows in her eyes lifted. She was mine now. I wondered what I would do with her.

Vasile

"THE PURPOSE OF THAT meeting was to reassure the other clans, not mess things up worse," Priest said later that day.

I'd gone to Familie, the bar and restaurant that also was the base of Clan Petran operations. Priest had arrived before me, and now he stood, deceptively casual in his stance, his face betraying nothing of what he thought. Was he expressing genuine concern or testing me to see how I would respond to his meddling? With Priest, one could never tell, a fact that had served him well and made him the rarest of our community, one who had connections to everyone but formal ties to no one.

"Are you telling me how to run my business, Priest?" I asked, deciding that whatever his intention, I would not be questioned, not by him or anyone else.

"I wouldn't, but more than your business is at stake here," he said. "Ashmore washes for your clan and four others, the Peruvians, the Sicilians, and the street gangs. If things are bad with him, things are bad with the money, and people die when things are bad with the money."

"Our arrangement stands," I said. "We'll send one hundred thousand per week, just as we always have."

Priest blinked rapidly, which was about as lively as he got. "So that simple, eh? That woman you stole doesn't matter?"

"I didn't steal her. He offered, tried to give her to me. I accepted," I said, allowing myself a grim smile, the memory of last night sparking anger anew. The woman—Fawn—shouldn't have been with that *porcine* in the first place.

"He tells a different story."

"Did he call you to complain, convince you to try to talk some sense into me?"

Priest laughed then, the sound surprisingly genuine. "I wouldn't waste my time trying to talk sense into a Petran. But remember how deep the ties between your families run. Your father worked with his—"

"My father is dead. His father is in jail. The decision is mine to make now," I said flatly.

"Why go to all this trouble for some whore?"

"Watch your tongue, Priest," I said, voice low, menacing.

I couldn't say why, but I didn't like him talking about Fawn that way. It reminded me of how Ashmore had treated her and made me want to forget my obligations and go make him regret doing so. That desire should have unnerved me, but it didn't, and I didn't have time to question why.

"No offense, Vasile. I'm only asking," he said.

"I don't answer to you, Priest," I responded.

"No you don't, but if this gets out of hand, you will have to answer to much worse," he said.

"So be it," I said.

"God, you Petrans. So stubborn."

I let out a quick smile and then turned serious. "And this is my opportunity," I said.

"How?"

"You think I don't hear the whispers, don't know how their minds work? They are itching to try me, see if I'm as tough as my father. And if I back down now, you know it won't be long until someone else tries to take advantage."

Priest nodded.

"So forget the other clans, the Peruvians, the Sicilians, the street gangs, Ashmore. I'm keeping her."

6

Vasile

As I DID MOST days, I'd stayed at Familie to handle business and later that afternoon, I sat in the private back room where Clan Petran met. Natasha Florescu walked toward me, drawing the appreciative gazes of the men who watched wherever she went. I understood why; her long black hair, slim yet shapely figure, flawless features, and wide blue eyes made her an attention-grabbing package. And that she was clan, the daughter of a respected soldier, one who had ultimately died rather than snitch, only enhanced her appeal.

When she reached me, she settled atop my lap, the small curves of her ass pressing against my knee. She also didn't mind using her looks and status to take liberties that others wouldn't be allowed, something I wasn't in the mood to indulge today, at least not too much.

"Whatever will you do with your new toy?" she asked.

It wasn't at all surprising that she, and everyone else in the room probably, knew what had happened just hours ago. I gave her a lot of leeway out of respect to her father, but not even Natasha's looks, nor her ties to my brother gave her the freedom to test me so.

"Natasha..." I said, letting the warning hang.

Her little smile dropped, but she recovered quickly, laying a hand on my chest. "Vasile, you know I worry about you," she said.

"Don't. And get off me," I said, dismissing her.

"Some men would pay a fortune, give their lives for the pleasure of me sitting on their lap," she said, eyes sparkling, completely undeterred and instead tossed a huge smile, one that had broken more hearts than she could probably count.

"I'm not some men," I said, and I wasn't. But I wasn't dead either, and recognized Natasha's beauty. In the past, I had respected her father and my brother too much to go there, and today, I couldn't shake the thought of how Fawn would feel this close to me, how her fuller curves would fill my arms, and I needed to keep those thoughts at bay.

I'd kept my voice flat, my gaze on hers, and

with a final slight nod, she stood.

"Wait for me. I have something for you to do," I said.

"Fine," she said.

Then she walked away, her heels clicking against the wood floor. I usually paid such things no attention, but watching Natasha again reminded me of Fawn, of how she'd managed to move so gracefully on those high heels. Natasha paused momentarily and tossed a mysterious smile at my brother as he entered and then continued.

"*Salut, frate,*" Sorin said as he came to stand in front of me, giving me a somewhat formal greeting, though his expression showed the underlying depth of our relationship.

"You seem in a good mood," I said.

"I had a good night's work," he said, and then he sat next to me and waved a hundred dollar bill at the waitress, who soon returned with a single glass and full bottle.

His smile spread from ear to ear and after quickly tossing back his first shot, he poured another. It didn't take much to get Sorin in a good mood, but I'd have to get details later, when we were alone and on safer ground. I turned toward him, catching the grin that still covered his face.

"Did Priest try to talk you out of it?" Sorin asked.

"Sorin, you speak in riddles and I have no energy to translate," I said. My voice was harsh, but my brother knew there were no teeth behind it. He was many things, many bad things, but he was my brother, and I would never let anything come between us.

"You stole the accountant's girl. I know he had something to say about it."

"I answer to no man," I said, echoing the words I'd said to Priest earlier.

Sorin smiled and nodded, then looked toward the front door. "You might have to answer to that," he said.

I watched as Ashmore approached, still dressed impeccably, but even in the dim light of the room, his eyes were shifty with energy and animation. Only the presence of the person who accompanied him kept me from dismissing him.

Vargas, one of the most powerful men in the city's criminal underworld.

Sorin stood, as did I. Priest's place was the neutral spot where factions met to discuss business or on occasion, relax without fear of reprisal. But Familie belonged to Clan Petran, was in the heart of my territory. This intrusion would not go unnoticed and could not go unremarked.

Ashmore rushed toward me and then stopped. "I want her back. Now!"

At his sharp-voiced words, people began filing out of the room, first the women and staff, then the men, and finally higher-level soldiers. They knew when to make themselves scarce, and a visit from Ashmore and the Peruvian definitely qualified as one of those times.

Sorin moved closer to Ashmore, close enough to the other man's face he could bite off his nose if he so chose. Something he'd done to others before.

"Do you know where you are?" Sorin asked.

The edge in his voice was razor-sharp, and he kept his eyes glued on Ashmore, waiting for the other man to do anything that would give him an excuse.

Vargas raised a hand, an attempt to placate Sorin. "We do. No disrespect intended. My associate is a little emotional."

"Are you sanctioning this intrusion, Vargas?" I asked.

He headed the sizable Peruvian faction, and was personally responsible for half of the city's drug trade. A person of his power in David's corner was surprising, but even Vargas's power would not sway me. If anything, this display only confirmed I'd done the right thing.

He shook his head. "Don't think of it that way. I'm simply facilitating a meeting, hopefully one between friends."

"He's no friend of mine." I inclined my head toward Ashmore. "You either. But we make money together. That can change," I said.

Vargas's eyes flashed with malice before he put his docile mask back in place. And that was all it was, the thinnest veneer of civility to hide the savagery underneath. It had helped him, too, his appearance of calm allowing him to emerge from the last war on top of the heap. It was impressive how he'd managed to pull rival factions together, wrangle complete control, and still maintain his reputation as a concilia- tor despite the bodies he'd stacked.

He'd worked hard for status, had gone to great lengths to keep it, and I wondered how deep his ties to David went if he was willing to risk it, or whether this was a surface play, a roundabout way for Vargas to solidify his hold on the Peruvians, which would give him al- most a monopoly on the drug trade and the money and power that came with it, a result I wouldn't allow.

I couldn't immediately read his intentions. Unlike so many others, Vargas was usually in control of his emotions, and his thin face, dark eyes gave away nothing.

"Business is business, and what you did was bad business," Vargas said, just manag- ing to stay on the right side of chiding, but only barely.

Sorin stepped closer to Vargas, his own tol- erance for the type of question Vargas posed far less than mine. But then again, Sorin had never been patient and had never, *ever*, over- looked a slight. That hotheaded nature always threatened to strike.

"Sorin, let Mr. Ashmore plead his case," I said.

Sorin recognized the play for what it was, the barest attempt to give Vargas at least some of what he wanted, and he went along with it, loosening his stance but still alternat- ing his glare between the two interlopers with naked contempt.

"Just give her back," Ashmore said, voice now a whine. "No harm, no foul. And I can sweeten the pot. I'll clean for free this week."

He looked at me hopefully, eyes half begging, half defiant before he choked out, "She can stay another day if you're not finished with her yet."

I thinned my lips and exhaled hard, my hands clenching into fists, anger at his continued mistreatment of her surging through my blood. Sorin glared at Ashmore harder, and even Vargas shot him a brief look of disdain.

"Do not come here again. Either of you," I said, looking at Vargas then.

"Please...I need her!" Ashmore cried, his hands balled into tight fists. "I need her."

"Mr. Petran, extending this courtesy is something my organization would look kindly on," Vargas said.

I huffed a breath and glared at Vargas. Of course his organization would look kindly on it. Why wouldn't it? Giving her back would be a show a weakness on my part and would solidify his relationship with Ashmore. It was an excellent outcome for him, which was probably why he'd risked coming here in the first place.

"Do not come here again," I said, keeping my eyes on Vargas, reminding him without words that he existed at the pleasure—and mercy—of Clan Petran. Yes, he'd displayed a savvy and brutality that was impressive, but had my clan taken sides, he would not have won. Seemed he'd forgotten that fact momentarily, but if the calculation I saw spinning in his eyes was a clue, he was quickly remembering.

"Thank you for your time. I hope we didn't disrupt your evening," Vargas finally said.

Then he turned, and Ashmore peered at him, mouth gaped open. "What about...?"

Vargas looked back. "You heard the man. And if you want to continue breathing, I suggest you follow me."

Now Ashmore's expression was a mix of anger, desperation, and fear. I focused on the fear, and twisted my face into an even more unwelcoming grimace.

"Just...tell her to please call me," he said, voice reminiscent of a little boy's, filled with hope and trepidation. He'd taken such pleasure in lording over her, of showing me how powerful he was because he controlled her. And now he was begging for a phone call that would never come. Pathetic, even more so than I'd pegged him for.

I stared at him silently, unblinking, and eventually, Ashmore turned and fled, trailing behind Vargas.

When they'd exited, Sorin relaxed his stance. "We should have fucked them up."

"It wasn't worth it," I replied.

"But pussy is worth fucking with our business?"

I clenched my fists tighter.

"You talk too fucking much, Sorin," I said sharply.

He froze, his expression flashing an apology before his features turned down into a frown. "Sorry, brother."

Then he left as well, probably in search of more drinks and women to pick up his celebration where it had left off. And when Priest returned, I simply shook my head, not the least bit surprised he was here. He regarded me with sharp black eyes, ones that practically demanded an explanation.

"That doesn't work on me," I said on a deep, tired sigh.

"I hope you know what you're doing, Vasile," he said as he sat next to me. "Rock the boat and you'll get splashed by the waves."

7

Fawn

HIS PLACE—I ASSUMED it was an apartment, maybe a town house, but there didn't seem to be any neighbors around—had been quiet, still, and I feared I might go mad from the whirling thoughts buzzing through my brain. Was it insane to stay with him, more insane than trying to avoid David? Was I really so weak I needed to hide behind a stranger? At least I knew the answer to that question was a resounding yes, and I wasn't ashamed, not really. The risk of David finding me was too great; I'd stay as long as Vasile let me.

That realization gave me peace, and some-how I had managed to sleep. The comfort of knowing David wasn't here, wouldn't burst in yelling about some slight or another while I slept allowed me to rest, really rest, more than I had since the day I'd met him all those years ago.

I woke slowly, my mind coming to wakefulness piece by piece, not immediately snapping into thought about how I would evade punishment. After stretching languorously, I walked toward the bathroom, the solitude and quiet of this place welcome now and not something that made me fearful. That would change when he came home.

"Vasile Petran."

Though I was alone, I said his name out loud, let the foreign sounds roll across my tongue. My pronunciation wasn't quite right, and I couldn't make my voice mimic the smooth way the name had fallen from his lips, but I smiled anyway at the little sizzle of warmth that lighted through me when I said it.

Feeling surprisingly buoyant, I stared at myself in the mirror. It hadn't even been twenty-four hours, but even I could see the difference in myself. I looked unburdened. For the first time in years, I could breathe. And all because of Vasile.

I looked around the nice but spartan bathroom and found thick black towels folded neatly. I grabbed one, stepped into the shower, and as the ice-cold and then steaming-hot water blasted me, I scrubbed myself. Wiped the remnants of makeup from my face. Shampooed my hair, uncaring I'd have no way to tame the mass of twisted curls once it dried. Washed every inch of my sienna-colored skin until it was raw and deep red under brown, unconcerned with the abrasions, not if it meant eliminating every trace of David.

A cliché, ridiculous even, but after I finished, I felt as if I was almost Fawn again and not whatever zombie David had constructed.

Of course, the newly emerged Fawn did not have anything to wear, something I didn't consider until I stood naked in the middle of his bathroom floor. With barely a glance at the black dress, I dismissed it immediately. Never again would anything of David's touch me.

I stepped into the main living area, more than halfway hoping a fully stocked closet would materialize. When that didn't happen, I turned my gaze to the drawer from which Vasile had taken the T-shirt. I walked toward it slowly, unsure what to do. I didn't want to intrude or snoop. There was no way I would ever cross a man like him, but even more, I didn't want to betray his kindness with invasion.

Still...as nice as his towels were, they weren't quite cutting it and left a thigh, hip, and breast mostly uncovered. It probably wasn't a problem for him. I bet the towels fit around his trim waist with ease, but I had no such luck. I chuckled at the thought and then headed to the dresser. Without looking too closely, I groped at the garments and pulled out another black T-shirt and a pair of underwear.

I threw on both garments quickly, worried the tight squeeze of the underwear on my hips would call attention to my ass, that the thin material of the T-shirt would put more emphasis on my unrestrained breasts. But then I shrugged and laughed again when my breasts moved. My curves didn't need attention called to them, so what I wore wouldn't make a difference. This would have to do, though I didn't dare look in the mirror.

Moments later, there was a firm knock at the door and then the *click* of the lock. I stood in the middle of the floor, feet bare, dressed in his underwear and waited. Vasile didn't strike me as a person who knocked, especially not in his own home, but I appreciated it, found that something so simple bolstered my belief that maybe, possibly, at least for a little while, I'd be safe here.

His gaze found me instantly, and he watched, face unreadable. I was struck with the impulse to pat my hair, turn my shoulders in as if that would somehow help me escape his intense gaze. It wasn't uncomfortable, but being looked at like that, like I was a person and not a possession wasn't something I was used to.

Long, commanding strides carried him to the dresser, and I spoke quickly. "I'm sorry. I didn't mean to snoop. I just needed something to wear."

His back was to me now, his shoulders impossibly broad, his entire being impossibly formidable, and more importantly in this moment, making it impossible for me to tell what he was doing. The fear that had receded started to come back. I couldn't tell what he was thinking when he looked at me, but seeing his face comforted me somehow, and with his back turned to me, I could tell nothing, was left to the mercy of my rising fear.

"Come here," he said, his back still turned, his voice icy.

I approached, each step making my heart beat faster until it boomed when I finally reached him.

"Wear this," he said, nodding at a pair of black jogging pants and black socks.

My knees weakened with my relief, and I quickly grabbed them and put them on, the fit poor, but at least they covered me more.

Then he shoved a stack of bills into my hands. "Natasha will take you to buy clothes. The car is outside."

And just that quickly, my relief fled and my heart dropped into my stomach. I looked down at the bills in my hands, bitter disappointment, strong and surprising, stirring in my chest. He'd rid me of David's costume and now he was going to replace it with his own.

"Is there something in particular you'd like?" I asked on a quiet whisper.

I'd learned nothing over the years, had let a few hours of soft treatment erase years of lessons. But I knew what I was good for, all that I was good for, and it was stupid of me to—

"Did you hear me?"

His voice broke into my thoughts, and I

turned my eyes to him, watching as he watched me.

I shook my head.

"Buy whatever you like," he said.

And then he walked into the bathroom, leaving me alone.

I again stared at the wad of bills in my hands, even more confused now than I'd been before.

And even worse, I wondered if I remembered what I liked. It had been so long since anyone, including myself, had asked what I liked that I was very much out of practice.

But the car was waiting, so, wearing only socks I had gotten from him, I made my way outside.

∭

Fawn

A SLICK BLACK LIMO sat next to the car that I'd arrived here in, and as I walked toward it, curiosity sparked. I had no idea who Natasha was and was more than intrigued as I opened the door and got inside the dark interior of the limo.

The first thing I saw was the ravishingly beautiful woman who sat regally, back straight, dark hair cascading down her shoulders in luxurious waves, head tilted to show her features in their most flattering light. I'd met women like her before, but few who could pull off her aura so convincingly.

"It's good that we're going shopping. You need it," she said, her voice softly accented.

Her words were matter-of-fact, almost cruel, but I felt strangely comforted, especially when she flashed a quick smile, one that I returned.

"I do," I said as the limo pulled off. "I'm Fawn."

She nodded. "Interesting name. It fits you. I am Natasha."

"Pleased to meet you," I said.

She quirked a brow, and I smiled. It was true. I wasn't exactly pleased, but for some reason, I wasn't displeased either. "Where are we going?" I asked.

"I think you don't want to dress like that," she said, indicating my cobbled-together outfit.

"No." I shook my head. "No I don't."

"We'll find something that you like then. Him too," she said mischievously, looking at me with an expression that dared me to contradict her implication.

I clenched my mouth shut, and she must have picked up on the change for she smiled a bit brighter.

"You don't want him?"

I looked away from her piercing blue gaze, choosing to ignore the question. I didn't know what I felt. He scared the crap out of me, but he'd been kind to me. And I couldn't deny his physical appeal.

"It's okay. It's just us girls," she whispered as if she was trying to coax secrets from me.

"You talk this way about your husband with other women?" I said, expressing the realization that had just occurred to me.

Then I closed my mouth again quickly, cursing myself for having spoken out of turn.

But Natasha simply laughed, her small frame moving with the sound. "You think he...? That Vasile is my husband?" she asked.

I nodded faintly, which triggered another wave of laughter.

"No. He is not mine or anyone else's. Never will be."

I told myself that the relief that filled me was simply because I had spared her the insult of what could only be the reasonable conclusion of me leaving his home dressed in his clothes. It was simply that and nothing else.

The conversation was mercifully cut short when the limo pulled to a stop.

"We're here," she said, stepping out of the car. I followed suit, but felt clumsy and unwieldy next to her.

She walked toward a small boutique, and I watched as an older woman opened the door and ushered us in.

When we entered, I looked around the place, one of those fancy stores that seemed mostly empty. And when I glanced at the clothes that hung on the racks, embarrassment slithered up my spine.

"Natasha." She turned, eying me patiently. "This stuff won't fit me," I said.

She looked me up and down, letting her

gaze caress my body. "I'll handle it. Eat," she said, gesturing toward the platter of fruit, crackers, and cheese that was laid out on a nearby table.

My stomach rumbled, but the embarrassment fled in the face of suddenly ravenous hunger. It had been nearly more than a day since my last meal. I headed for the table.

8

Fawn

"NO, NATASHA," I SAID.

At the sight of her pouty expression, I almost giggled, but managed to hold firm. She held the chiffon negligee in front of her as if doing so would convince me.

"You have the assets for it," she said, lowering her gaze to linger on my breasts and hips. "You could seduce any man in this." She added a hilarious waggle of her eyebrows to the end of the sentence.

"I'm not trying to seduce anyone," I said.

"Of course you are. It's the way we survive," she said turning solemn, and while I didn't want to acknowledge it, there was truth in what she said.

After I'd unapologetically stuffed myself with fruit and crackers and watched Natasha polish off half a bottle of champagne, which seemed to have no effect at all, I had begun to enjoy my time with her, laughing at her outrageous suggestions, amused by her quick wit, able to pretend for just a little while I was a normal girl out with a friend and not ensnared in a world of darkness, that I was more than a commodity.

But that enjoyment was lessened at the cold reality of Natasha's words. I knew better than most, probably even her, that my value was only measured by the pleasure that I gave, the pain I could withstand. And this little excursion, as fun as it had been, would not change that. I was as I had always been: a man's property. That I'd chosen to be so willingly this time, even though I'd sworn that if I ever got away from David I'd never belong to anyone again, sent a rush of shame through me.

"Don't be sad, Fawn," she said, laying a hand on my shoulder, the act a representation of how we'd become fast friends. "He can be very kind."

"Cruel too," I said, a statement and not a question.

"Very. But sometimes and only when given cause."

"And he decides what's cause?"

She nodded. "But it is always that way for women like us."

"Like us?" I asked, some of my dour mood

fading at the hope I might have found a kin-
dred spirit.

Natasha regarded me. "Like us. Your last
one, he was very bad, yes? Bad enough that
Vasile took you?"

I nodded, though I couldn't say for sure
why he'd done what he had.

"I haven't suffered as much as you, but it's
the same. Vasile takes care of me now, but it's
just a matter of time until I belong to another.
I just hope that when it finally happens, it's
someone I want, not whoever is around."

She looked at me then, seeming younger,
almost naive, so different than her coquettish
speech and demeanor suggested. "Your father,
did he give you to the man who had you before
Vasile?"

If only it had been so simple. If only I had
someone other than myself, something other
than my own naïveté and stupidity to blame.

"I'd rather not talk about it," I finally said,
breaking her gaze.

She nodded, patted my shoulder. "Maybe
one day."

I doubted it, but I nodded.

"So this is all you're going to buy?"

I looked down at the small pile of clothing.
A couple of pairs of jeans, some Capri pants, a
few underthings, and long-sleeved T-shirts.
"Yes. It's more than enough."

"As you wish. We should return," she said.

She patted my hand one last time.

55

Vasile

"WHERE IS SHE?" SORIN asked as he practically barreled past me to get inside, looking around the room like an eager puppy.

"I sent Fawn out with Natasha. Oleg is driving," I said.

"Fawn? What kind of name is that?" he asked.

"Why are you here, Sorin?" I replied, changing the subject.

He nodded, and in an instant went serious, eyes going from laughing dark blue to deadly focused.

"What you suspected was right," he said, voice laced with venom.

"You've confirmed it?" I asked.

"Personally. Do you want me to handle it?"

I shook my head. "I'll take care of it. Have everyone gather day after tomorrow," I said.

"You're going to make him sweat," he said, eyes gleaming with malice.

"If he's done nothing wrong, he'll have no reason to sweat. And if he has..." I shrugged.

"What if he runs?" Sorin asked.

"Then I'll chase him down like the dog that he is. And besides, he has already disgraced his family name. Do you think he would bring further shame to them?"

"You never know," Sorin said.

"You don't," I agreed.

This was an unfortunate truth of the business. Most of Clan Petran were strong, solid, respected our rules and traditions. And if nothing else, this would be a good reminder for them to continue to do so.

"What else?" I asked, noting the tension that still radiated from Sorin.

"Vargas has consolidated the rest of the Peruvians. He's effectively distributing for the entire city," he said as he retrieved a beer from the refrigerator and leaned against the counter.

"And?" I asked, knowing where this conversation was headed.

"And that wasn't what the clans agreed to."

"We've never been in the business of managing others, Sorin. What the Peruvians do is not our concern unless it becomes our concern," I said.

"Even after Vargas disrespected you?" he asked scornfully.

"Yes, even after."

"You shouldn't let that go," Sorin grumbled.

I shook my head. "You're grown now. Act like it, and use your brain. If Vargas had gone too far, I would have handled it, but what do I get by interfering now?"

"For one, you'd make sure everyone knows not to fuck with Clan Petran. And it's stupid to give up all that money," he said.

"Everyone knows not to fuck with us. And drug money, Sorin."

"Yeah, drug money is money," he said,

looking at me indignantly.

We'd had this conversation countless times, and I hadn't ever budged.

"Think. What would we have to gain by taking that business?"

"Money," he said as if the answer was self-evident.

"And what would we have to lose?" I asked, raising the same point I had so often before.

Sorin went silent, his clenched jaw flexing. It was always that way with him. He rarely thought about consequences, infrequently slowed to consider the repercussions.

I broke the silence. "Why would we take the risk of the Peruvian drug operation when we can let them do all the work and get 15 percent of the profits?"

"Fifteen percent is nothing. We could have more," he said.

"And it would never be enough. How many other clans thought the same, started with the drug trade, only to disintegrate? How many proud families have been brought to their knees by greed and infighting over pieces of the drug pie? That won't happen to Clan Petran. Not while I'm in charge. I'm going to prove it the day after tomorrow, but I'm reminding you now."

Sorin took another swallow and tilted his head, as much of an acknowledgment as he'd give me, I knew. But I didn't need to belabor the point. We'd seen it happen countless times, had lost our father in the crossfire of such a skirmish.

"And it's not like we're in the poor house. We have fights, the clubs, the rent," I said.

"That shit's boring," he said.

"We don't do this for excitement, Sorin."

"You don't," he replied.

"That's right. My baby brother does it so that he can beat people up and chase girls. That's the exciting life you love, eh?"

I crossed the room and clapped him on the shoulder, his exuberance lightening my spirit like always, even when he was being a troublemaker.

"Those are perks," he said with a smile before he again turned serious. "I know why we do it."

"Because we are clan," I said, echoing words that had filled our ears since birth.

A faint, timid knock at the door broke the moment. Sorin's eyes flashed with excitement.

"She's here!" he exclaimed.

"Why are you so excited?" I asked.

"She got your attention. *Yours.* My brother, who is so detached he barely seems alive, the one who hasn't looked at a woman in as long as I can remember. I have to see her," he said.

He bounded across the room and opened the door, but I stayed in place. Sorin was right. I did avoid attachments, kept focused on my business. And I still hadn't figured out what about her had made me break from that pattern.

"Oh!"

Fawn's soft exclamation was followed by Natasha's impatient huff.

"Let us in, Sorin," she said.

"Yeah, yeah."

He moved aside, and Fawn entered carrying three bags. I couldn't help but look at her, the conservative jeans and T-shirt she wore so different, but so much better than that ridiculous black dress.

"Thank you, Natasha," I said before she came in. "Oleg will take you home."

A fleeting disappointment filled her expression but then she smiled that trademark seductive grin. "Of course. It was lovely, Fawn," she said and then left.

"A beautiful name," Sorin said, grinning from ear to ear.

Fawn just looked up at him, expression wary. If Sorin noticed, he didn't care, and instead pulled her into a brief hug, kissed each of her cheeks, and then rested his hands on her shoulders, openly assessing her. I was prepared to intervene, the look of shock on Fawn's face driving me toward them, but Sorin dropped his hands from her shoulders.

"I am Sorin Petran, the handsome brother. It is an honor to meet you," he said.

"Day after tomorrow," I called in Romanian, and Sorin nodded.

"Good-bye, Fawn," he said, and then she and I were alone.

She blinked and then turned back to the door before looking at me again.

"Sorin is...excitable, but harmless," I said, choosing to expand the truth for her benefit.

Her eyes widened.

"What is it?" I asked.

She looked down sharply.

"Fawn, what is it?" I repeated.

Her lips turned up and she met my eyes. "You smile when you talk about him," she said.

Almost automatically, I raised my hand to my face and found that I had indeed begun to smile, and it occurred to me Sorin might not be the reason. A troubling development, and one I would ignore for the moment.

"Is that all you bought?" I asked.

She nodded. "Yes." Then she walked toward me, fumbling in her jeans' pocket. "Here," she said when she'd retrieved the cash. "Your change."

I waved it away.

"No. Please," she said. "It's a lot, and if I add that, it'll take me even longer to pay you back. I still haven't figured out how I'm going to start."

She hooded her eyes then, the huskiness of her voice having created an implication she hadn't intended, one that I hadn't realized until just this moment I might like.

"Keep it," I said firmly.

We stood for moments longer, Fawn clearly warring with whether to object, but she finally relented. "I will pay you back," she said with the most certainty I'd ever heard her say anything.

"As you wish," I said.

Later, when it was time to sleep, she looked at the bed and then me, eyes wary as they'd been the night before. It angered me.

"If I wanted to rape you, I could have a

thousand times over," I said in a gruff voice that was a near growl.

She looked stricken, and then to my surprise, apologetic. "I—It's just that, people always want things."

"People like me?" I asked, voice scornful.

She nodded. "Yes. People like you. And people like David. Nothing in this life is free, Vasile," she said, sounding both wise and weary, something that made me want to hold her close and protect her because I knew what she said was true. The instinct was completely foreign to me, one I didn't dare act on but one that I couldn't ignore either.

"Don't say his name here," I said.

She immediately nodded her assent, and I continued, "You can take care of this place to repay me."

"Okay." She smiled and nodded almost happily. Then she closed the distance between us but stopped before she reached me. She extended her hand slowly, let her fingers rest against my wrist for the briefest moment.

"Thank you, Vasile," she said. Then she moved quickly to climb into bed, the pants and long-sleeved T-shirt she wore quite different than yesterday's attire, but still doing nothing to disguise the lush curves of her body.

When she'd settled, she looked toward me expectantly.

"I'll sleep later," I said and then turned abruptly and headed to the bathroom.

I considered myself a logical man, one not

subject to emotions or raging passions, but Fawn was challenging that belief as the iron-hard erection her simple touch had spawned proved. Yes, she'd been through things, had shown glimpses of a woman familiar with the griminess of the world, something I respected, but this reaction to her was unexpected.

After working my pants around my cock and down, I got into the shower, hoping it would cool me.

It did not.

Thoughts of her full lips had me lifting my hand. Thoughts of the long column of her neck, the soft-looking skin there had me closing my hand around my shaft. And thoughts of the bounty of her body laid out before me, a near-endless series of curves and valleys to explore had me sliding my hand down for the first stroke.

Would she be tentative, shy, when I touched her, or would she touch me back? My cock leaked precum furiously, my own fluid mixing with the cold spray of the shower and slicking my hand as I stroked myself harder and then harder, imagining Fawn's warm body under mine, her wide eyes looking up at me as I pounded into her.

My orgasm hit hard and fast, cum shooting out of me on a rush of gut-wrenching pleasure. I leaned against the cool tile and rode out my climax. Once I finally regained conscious thought, I wondered what I'd gotten myself into.

9

Fawn

"DO YOU LIKE IT?"

I waited by the stove, watching him intently as he sat at his table, the shadows created by the falling darkness making his always inscrutable face even more so.

He murmured a few low, indecipherable words and then took another bite, not looking at me, focused on the plate I had anxiously set in front of him minutes ago.

"I can make something else," I said, nerves springing up in my stomach.

"It's fine." His voice was flat, as icy as it had been that first day, and my nerves redoubled.

Twisting my hands together, I drifted closer to where he sat at the table and speaking around the building tightness in my throat, I said, "I wasn't sure what you wanted, so I made this, but I can—"

Green eyes as hard as shards of crystal silenced me. "I said it was fine."

His lips were a flat line, the thunderous expression on his face making me huff out a harsh breath, my lungs growing tight with fear. I'd done something, and I racked my brain trying to figure out what it was and what I needed to do to fix it.

Vasile stood and carried his plate to the kitchen sink, his big body coiled tight with tension. I didn't move, wished that I could sink into the floor to escape the intensity—and fear—of this moment. He turned then and walked toward me, eyes still icy cold, and for reasons I couldn't articulate, I stepped back again and again until I could go no farther.

As he pierced me with his stare, I thought I might explode from the tension, and when he finally spoke, a shriek slipped out before I could stop it.

"Are you afraid of me, Fawn?" he asked, face close to mine, voice low, dangerous, arousing.

I met his gaze and lied. "No."

"You should be."

Not even a breath passed before he closed the scant distance between us, his lips so close to mine that the faintest movement would have made our mouths touch. But he stayed back, mouth millimeters from mine, his warm breath sparking a wave of shivers. His expression was still harsh, but this close, his lips were surprisingly soft-looking, and the thought of him touching me with them left me light-headed with desire, which contrasted with the fear that had ebbed but was still there.

I twisted my head, and my cheek brushed against his mouth. It was a light touch, barely a caress, but that simple touch was enough to capture me. His power had never been in question, but that contact with his skin made me want to give all of myself to him, to give in to the pull that had been there from my very first glimpse of him.

As if of their own volition, my hands crept up, the touch of his hard biceps against my palms, the sizzle of his smooth, hot skin making me suck in a quick breath. He turned his eyes to meet mine, and I dropped my hands.

He stared at me, his eyes icy, his face twisted cruelly, but his breath coming out harshly. Slowly, he raised his hand and stroked it down my cheek, across the column of my throat, down the middle of my chest to rest between my breasts, his hard, heavy hand flat against me. He pushed me gently until I was flush against the wall and then kept his hand there.

I wondered if he felt my heart pounding against his hand, and then all thought fled when he moved again, sliding his hand down my stomach to rest on my waistband. Eyes still on mine, he lifted his other hand and deftly opened my pants and pushed them down to midthigh. On instinct, I tried to widen my stance but my pants held me hostage, as did the almost chiding look that sparked in his eye.

I went still and waited, breath hanging as I watched him, wondering what he would do. That fear and uncertainty remained, but more, I wanted him to touch me.

Badly.

And when he finally did, I cried out, the deep, throaty moan that bubbled from me only giving a hint of the desperate desire that seemed to intensify with each passing second. His rough fingers against my pussy sparked pleasure, and I couldn't stop the ripple that rushed through me or the low, frenzied moans that poured from my throat.

His hand was huge, hot, rough yet gentle, and the dizzying sensations he stirred left me disoriented, torn between the desire—need—to seek more and the fear that I wouldn't be able to withstand it. That fear died on a choked-out moan, replaced with the insistent need for more when he pressed up, his palm pushing against my clit, the pressure intense but not nearly enough.

Eyes slammed shut, I groped out to feel him, his solid, heavy muscles under hot, smooth skin only ratcheting my need further. I didn't recognize the husky voice that spilled from me. I'd never made a sound like it. No one, certainly not David, had ever made me feel even a fraction of what he did. That was even more true when he worked his fingers against my slit, spreading my lips with easy but persistent caresses, ones that coaxed even more moisture from me with each pass.

He was a stranger, a terrifying, dangerous one, yet more than anything, I wanted him inside me. I rocked my hips, trying to get more, and he took pity on me and sped his motion, allowing one finger to ever so slightly breach me.

"Please... More..." I cried, gripping his thick, solid forearms tight.

I rocked against him harder, faster, trying to set a rhythm that would send me to the climax that lay within reach, but he moved at his own speed, driving me higher but not sending me over.

"Fawn."

My name on his lips, the low rumble of his voice, the accent that had once sounded cruel but now dripped over me like warm honey gave me the strength to open passion-heavy eyes. Our gazes collided, the icy green of his softer now, sparkling like the finest jewels. His expression was still stern, but I thought I could see desire in his huffed breaths and the tight clench of his jaw.

And then my eyes slammed closed again when he pushed two thick fingers inside me, filling me more than I ever had been before. One pump, two, and I clamped down on him, my cunt sucking at his fingers, trying to keep him inside. His harshly exhaled breath fanned across my face, and I was so sensitized that the simple touch felt like a heated caress.

Our bodies didn't touch except where I gripped his arms and where his fingers pumped inside me. He still hadn't even kissed me. But none of that mattered. No one had ever possessed me as fully as he did in this moment. And with that thought echoing in my mind, I held him as the pleasure rushed through me, cresting and then falling in a wave that had my vision blurring at the edges.

"Let me..." I started long, long moments later, laying a hand on the hard ridge that tented his pants, wanting to give him some of the pleasure he'd given me.

But he slipped his fingers from me, grasped my arm, lifted my hand, and placed a soft kiss on my wrist.

And then he was gone.

10

Vasile

"Do you want me to handle it?" Sorin asked.

"You wish," I said, allowing myself a moment of levity before we entered Familie. "But no. It's my responsibility."

Sorin nodded as we made my way to the back room. The restaurant was closed today, and only Clan Petran was present. I stared out at the men assembled, all of their faces familiar, men who had been here before me, some of whom would be here after I was gone. I centered my gaze on one in particular.

"Viktor," I said, the crowd quieting when I spoke, "is there something you need to tell me?"

Viktor kept his gaze averted, confirming what Sorin had discovered. I waited, and the room went silent, the moment tense and heavy. We all knew why we were here.

"I apologize," he finally said. "It won't happen again."

"What won't happen again, Viktor?" I asked.

"I won't sell drugs for the Peruvians again," he mumbled.

"Why not?" I asked.

"Because the leader of my clan has forbidden it."

"And you will make amends?" I asked.

"Of course," Viktor said, nodding. He looked up, his rugged, worn face almost hopeful.

Then he stepped from the crowd and laid his hand atop a table. He reached into his pocket and pulled out a serrated knife. I watched as he pushed down, removing his pinkie and ring finger in one clean slice.

And to his credit, Viktor didn't cry out. The only hint of any reaction was the flash of pain that crossed his face and the shudder that passed through his body. He then took a handkerchief from his pocket and wrapped it around his bleeding hand, the blood that flowed from his fingers wetting the fabric almost instantly.

"Is that your amends?" I asked, stepping closer to Viktor.

He nodded. "Is it sufficient?" he asked, still hopeful.

"It is not," I said. Then I plucked the knife from his fingers and slashed it across his throat, stepping out of the path of the blood that spurted from the wound. I watched as he fell to his knees, a gurgling sound emerging from his throat as he groped at the wound, fingers going slick with his blood.

He collapsed completely to the ground, twitching, and I watched until he moved no more.

"That is the only amends for betrayal," I said, meeting the eye of every man in the room. I saw understanding in some faces, fear in others, but all received the message. Betrayal would not be tolerated.

After a moment, Oleg and Sorin grabbed Viktor and carried him out as the others turned their attention back to me.

"Is there other business that needs to be discussed?" I asked.

No one spoke, so I nodded, and the men broke into their groups. Soon, boisterous laughter and animated conversation filled the room, much like any other day.

It wasn't though. Viktor had been well liked, and some might take his death hard. And those who didn't would still be watching, searching for any sign of weakness, any hint of second-guessing.

There would be none, but I needed to stay, make my presence felt, and root out any dissension before it could fester. I moved among the men, congratulating one on the birth of a third son, another on his wedding, gave my condolences to yet another on the loss of cousin in a territorial dispute and reassured him that the perpetrators would be handled. It came naturally enough. I'd watched my father, his father, do much the same thing all my life, and yet I wondered...

I didn't feel guilty about killing Viktor. It had been necessary, and death, that of others and even my own, was a part of my life I had come to terms with years ago. But I couldn't help but think of Fawn, of how she would react if she knew what I'd done, what I was.

The thought was something that nagged at the back of my mind. The swine I had taken her from was low, but I doubted he'd ever gotten his hands dirty. But mine were, and they would never be clean. Could I touch her with them again?

Would I be able to not?

"Vasile."

Priest pulled me from my thoughts as he approached.

"Not a friendly visit," I said.

As usual, Priest's demeanor was closed, mysterious, but he didn't drop by for social calls. This was about business.

"I hope all of my visits are friendly, but I've come with a message. Or rather, a request."

He had my interest. Priest was no errand boy, so this had to be important, and I thought I could guess the subject.

"What is it?" I asked.

"Vargas asked me to extend a dinner invitation. He'd like to open his doors and welcome you into his home, an apology for his intrusion.

He hopes to bury any animosity between you and Ashmore."

I couldn't tell what Priest thought of all this, but it was a bold move on Vargas's part, either an attempt to further solidify his position among the Peruvians or to test me. Probably both, but I wouldn't be Vargas's pawn. If I rejected the invitation, it would be a sign of disrespect. If I accepted, it could be seen as a sign of weakness. But an idea sparked, and I nodded slowly at Priest.

"There's no animosity. And I accept."

"Good. We wouldn't want anything to disrupt operations."

"Always worried about the bottom line, Priest. What about honor?" I asked.

That got what passed for a smile from him. "There's no such thing. You know that by now, Vasile."

Fawn

WHEN HE CAME HOME, I didn't bother to pretend I was asleep. It felt...dishonest, and he'd have seen through it anyway. And, there was the fact that I wanted to see him, wanted to get back something of the connection we'd shared, if only for those brief moments.

But doing so had proved difficult. He'd been different, more distant, and I wondered if

KEEP

it was something I had done. I'd quickly come to feel comfortable here, safe, and I didn't want to jeopardize that. And though I tried to pretend otherwise, I was attracted to him. Stupid because I knew what he did, what he was, but I wanted him, and I thought he felt the same.

I tried to avoid those thoughts, recognized he wasn't prone to sentimentality, that whatever I'd felt that night had no reflection on what he had. It may have meant nothing to him, been a few moments of amusement. That felt wrong to me somehow. I was sure I'd seen something in his eyes, but as I'd proven, I was hardly a person who could rely on her perceptions. And Vasile's actions, his lack thereof, didn't clarify things one way or another. He hadn't touched me again, and I wasn't too proud to admit I'd missed his touch, craved it.

He went to the kitchen, not looking at me as usual.

"Vasile?" I called before I could stop myself, voice so weak I would not have been surprised if he hadn't heard me.

He looked toward me quickly, and I could see the tension in his face, in his stance, and it called to me. And I answered. Using courage I hadn't known I had, I walked toward him, my heart pounding with both fear and anticipation. I stopped when I stood in front of him, the heat from his body, his spicy, masculine scent making me want to touch him everywhere, breathe him in until he was all I felt, smelled, tasted. I didn't, though, and instead lifted my hand to his stubbled jaw. His eyes flashed, but he stayed still. I stroked his jaw, the coarse beginnings of the beard that he always seemed to sport rough against my fingers and making me imagine how it would feel on other parts of my body.

Brimming with boldness, I let my thumb graze his bottom lip, surprised by its masculine softness. He turned his face into a scowl, and pulled back.

"Don't, Fawn," he said, his voice a rough, husky whisper.

I ignored him and dragged my fingers lower, down his strong chin, the powerful column of his throat, a little trill flittering through me when he swallowed, and then lower over his collarbones, across his shoulders, over the tattoos that covered his biceps.

He grabbed my wrist and pulled my hands away, his eyes piercing mine. "You can't take this back, Fawn. We do this, and you're mine."

11

Vasile

WHAT I'D INTENDED AS a warning, she took as permission. A fact that became clear when she laid her free hand on my chest and tilted her head, slightly parting her full lips. I'd half hoped she would deny me, save me from my own desires because I was powerless against them. But now that she hadn't, I tossed aside my reservations about what this would mean for her and for me, and gave in to the need that had been building since the very first moment I laid eyes on her.

I dropped her wrist and snaked my arm around her waist and pulled her to me, her lush, soft body warm and full against me, a perfect fit. Then, breath coming in increasingly

harsh exhales, I moved toward her and captured her mouth with mine. Her lips were
softer than I'd imagined, warmer, and that
first touch had me anxious for her, so I deepened the kiss, moving my lips over hers with
increasing speed.

And she responded, kissing me back with a
fervor that surprised me along with a tight
grip on my arm. I'd seen and tried to ignore
the little flashes of desire in her eyes, had
halfway convinced myself that it was gratitude, or maybe a ploy to stay on my good side.

The way she kissed me now gave lie to that.
Her pounding heart, her sharp exhales, the
way she eagerly brushed her lips against mine,
none of it was born out of gratitude, and proof
of her desire only heightened mine.

I coaxed her lips apart with the tip of my
tongue and then delved into the warmth of her
mouth, the first touch of her tongue against
mine making both of us moan. As I kissed her,
I touched her body, moved my hands up her
strong back and then down again over the full
rounds of her ass and her thick thighs. I lifted, and she linked her legs around my waist,
her breasts crushed against my chest, her hot
core centered over my erection.

I enjoyed the feel of her weight in my arms
and then moved across the room and lay on
the bed, Fawn under me. I broke the kiss then
and looked down at Fawn. Her kiss-swollen
lips and passion-filled brown eyes stole my
breath, and when she snaked her fingers under

my shirt, her touch against my bare skin took what was left of my control.

I grabbed at the breasts that had become an increasingly prominent part of my obsession with her, squeezed at the full flesh that filled my hands, her tight nipples hard points against my palms.

My grip tightened when she pulled my shirt up, her fingers hot against my skin and leaving little ripples of pleasure with her touch. Desperate for more, I broke away, pulled the shirt off, and tossed it aside. I watched her eyes, looking for a response when she first glimpsed the tattoos that marked much of my skin.

But I saw nothing but desire in her eyes, felt it reflected in her soft, passionate touches. And when she looked up at me with pleading eyes, I couldn't do anything but respond.

I kissed her again, briefly, but then broke the kiss and pulled at her shirt, taking it and her bra in one motion. And then I stared down at her, smooth brown skin, succulent dark-tipped breasts calling out for my touch.

I answered, kissing my way over her collarbone and down her chest until I caught one of those hard buds in my mouth and teased the other between my fingers. She arched against me, and I smiled around her tit at her low moans, the way she groped at my shoulders only spurring me to tease that much harder.

Thumb tormenting one nipple, I used my tongue on the other, circling the bud and then sucking hard, repeating the motion until Fawn was a writhing mass beneath me. But she still had her wits about her, for as I sucked at her nipples, alternating between one and then the other, she somehow worked at my pants, got them open and down far enough to free my cock.

When she closed her fingers around me, I released her breast and cried out, her hot hand on my hardness making my dick jump. I exhaled, my breath against her wet nipple puckering the skin. I captured the bud again and then released, sucking at the underside of her breast, licking at the crease where her breast met her chest.

We continued that way, my shaft now wet with the precum that she'd spread with each stroke, but soon, the need for more pushed me on, and I broke away from her. Much as I had her shirt and bra, I quickly rid her of her pants and panties, exposing her long legs, the full thighs that had felt so good under my hands, to my eyes. They were a feast to my sight, as were her lovely hips, and the rise of her mound between them.

Some of the pleasure dampened as she watched me, and I could see the rising worry in her eyes, the trepidation about my response. I would see it replaced.

I kneeled beside her, my cock so hard it almost hurt, and without pause, I put my hand between her knees, moved up the smoothness of her thigh, drawing ever closer to the heat at her center. When I reached it, I put one finger between her lips, lifting one corner of my mouth at her sharp exhale, and then traced it up her slit, the need to bury myself in the warm heat I found there making my movements shaky.

When I reached her protruding clit, I stopped, caught her gaze with mine, happy her eyes had gone heavy-lidded with passion. Then I raised my hand to my lips, Fawn's sweet scent hitting my nose and then her even sweeter taste exploding across my tongue when I licked my wet finger. Then I pushed her legs wide, crawled between them, moving up her body until we were face-to-face, cock to pussy.

One hand on either side of her head, I kissed her, my dick resting right at the edge of her entrance. And then, mouth covering hers, I pressed inside her warm wetness, her tightness giving in to take me.

She breathed out, and I captured her exhale, returned one of my own, the feeling of her cunt stretching to accommodate me making my hands clench into tight fists, my body tense as I held back, trying to restrain myself.

But when Fawn broke the kiss, met my eyes, and then lifted her hips and pulled me deeper, that restraint snapped. In one thrust, I brought us together, her breath coming out in a rush, mine doing the same with our pelvic bones crashing together. And then, without pausing, I grasped her shoulders and moved, pulling out and then pounding in, Fawn's hands on my arms, my back, my ass, driving me harder, faster until my body was slick with sweat, my chest heaving with my breaths.

Her gaze never strayed from mine, not even when I reached between our bodies and circled her clit, pinched and teased it until she clamped down and cried out her pleasure. She didn't stray as she rode her climax, after as I continued to pound into her, or even after when, unable to hold back, I spilled my seed inside her.

12

Fawn

VASILE SAT ACROSS THE table from me, his expression almost serene but more detached than it had been less than an hour before when he'd again taken me to heights of pleasure I hadn't dreamed of. But though he was still mysterious, I saw a softness in his face I hadn't seen before.

"Natasha is coming today."

I brightened, excited at the prospect of seeing her again. "Great. Any reason?"

"She's bringing you a dress for tonight," he said.

"What's happening tonight?" I asked, frowning. He hadn't mentioned anything, and save a few trips to the grocery store, usually accompanied by Oleg, I hadn't gone out. And as strange as it may have been, I didn't welcome the prospect of changing things. I liked being in this little cocoon, me and Vasile and the passion between us, and while I knew it couldn't last, I didn't welcome the outside world's intrusion.

"We're going to dinner. I'll be back later to pick you up."

He was gone before I could think of a response and a few minutes later, Natasha burst into the room carrying two heavy garment bags.

"I brought these for you," she said, toddling over to me on her heels, face set into an almost gleeful smile. "I wasn't sure what would fit, so I got a couple things. We'll find something," she said.

I tilted my head in confusion. "Do you know what this is about?" I asked.

"Vasile said dinner, so I imagine it's business." She glanced at me, her expression turning down. "You've done this sort of thing before, yes?"

I nodded, swallowing down the disappointment that rose in my throat. After my initial reluctance, I'd begun to hope this mysterious "dinner" was something else, maybe a sign he cared for me, wanted to take me out. So stupid.

"Yes, I have," I finally said, memories of David, the countless evenings I'd spent playing the perfect hostess, the punishment for any mistake, racing through my mind.

"So you know what to do." She shrugged. "Just sit there and laugh when you should, don't offend anyone. It won't be hard."

Maybe not for her, but it was always hard for me. Always.

"Who went with him before?" I asked.

"Me, but it seems I've been replaced," she said, looking away as she unzipped the garment bag and then pulled out one dress. She eyed the garment. "Too much skin. We'll go with the other one."

"Natasha, I don't—"

"He's doing you a great honor, you know," she said, looking at me sympathetically.

"What honor? I get to dress up and make nice with a bunch of madmen," I said.

"You get to sit at the side of one of the most powerful men in the country. Do you know how many would kill for that seat?" she asked solemnly.

"They are welcome to it," I said. I'd been in a seat like it before, a showpiece, a measure of my owner's taste and worth, no different than a car or a house or a fancy piece of jewelry. I didn't want to ever be in it again, not even for him.

"They may be, but you said it yourself: we don't get to make that choice." Her expression shifted. "Now we have to get ready. We only have a few hours."

Fawn

"This is way too tight, Natasha," I said, looking at myself in the mirror and frowning at the sight of the material pulled tight across my breasts and behind.

"You're completely covered. Classy but desirable. Vasile will be pleased," she said, smiling like a proud mama.

I thinned my lips at her statement. At the moment, I couldn't care less what would please him and it seemed he felt the same, but I kept my thoughts to myself. "In the technical sense, you're right. But the long sleeves and a high neck don't change the fact this dress is so tight you can practically see my heartbeat," I said.

She laughed, staring at our reflections in the mirror. "You will be on the arm of Vasile Petran. No one will look above your ankles or below your chin," she said.

And she patted me on the shoulder. I grabbed her hand, wanting to thank her for her kindness, for making this whole thing much less awful than I knew it could have been.

"I'm glad you're going to be there."

She shrugged. "It might be fun. Someone's always amusing at these things, and Sorin might not be too obnoxious," she said nonchalantly, but I didn't miss the tightness around her mouth.

"Does he know?" I asked.

She turned her eyes toward me, a faint little smile playing at her lips. "Know what?"

"That you love him?"

She lifted the corner of her mouth again. "You think I'm in love with Vasile, that I'm jealous because you took my spot," she said.

I shook my head. "I know you are not in love with him. But Sorin, does he know?"

Her smile dropped, and for just an instant, I saw beyond her shiny facade, saw to the woman underneath, one who felt invisible to the man she loved.

"No, but it doesn't matter. I know what I mean to him, and he's always been honest with me."

"But you should—"

"Do what? Put my foot down? Tell him I won't let him use me? Make him commit?"

I stood silent, knowing that she was right. Sorin, Vasile, none of the men would do anything unless they wanted to. "You can't make him, but you don't have to..."

"But I want to, Fawn. I love him. And if sex is all he has to offer, I'll take it," she said, a tear slipping from her eye.

"Maybe one day he'll come to his senses," I offered, patting her thin hand.

"You've met Sorin, yes?" she replied, managing to shape her mouth into a smile.

I nodded.

"Then you know why I'm not counting on that," she said.

13

Vasile

I HAD ONLY JUST dressed, and already I wanted to rip the suit and tie from my body. I hated this, playing dress up like children. We all knew what we were, and I never understood the need to pretend to be something else.

But I'd agreed to this, and I'd get through it. Oleg opened the limo door, and Fawn entered, folding herself into the seat with ease and grace.

My heart began to pound as I watched her, sheathed by the tight dress that both covered and revealed, making the valleys and curves of her body apparent to anyone. I had half a mind to send her back, but I wanted her with me, needed to prove this point once and for all.

"Did you pick that?" I asked flatly.

She chuckled. "Not ever. This is Natasha's work."

"I'll have to talk with her."

"She was only trying to help like you asked," she said, but then she went quiet and stared out the window, watching as the city passed.

"I'm surprised she and Sorin aren't with us," she said after a while.

"He prefers his own transportation," I said.

I continued to watch her, her hands twisted, her face set in a placid expression I now knew concealed a deep well of insight. And though she tried to hide it, I also saw fear.

"You've been to this type of meeting before?" I asked.

She nodded. "Yes. Don't worry. I know how this goes. I won't embarrass you."

I frowned at her implication. "He will be there," I said.

Her eyes flew to mine, and I could see the panic spark in them.

"He cannot harm you. Won't even dare try," I said.

She was skeptical. Her expression said that and more. "You don't know him. He might try anything. I never know what," she said and then she looked away.

"Fawn."

Head still averted, she did not meet my eyes.

"Fawn," I repeated, voice firm. She finally turned to me.

"Do you know what happened when I took you, when you decided to stay?"

Her eyes widened, and she shook her head quickly.

"You came under my protection, under the protection of Clan Petran. No one will ever harm you. Ever."

At her sharp inhale, I looked down and realized I had clenched my fist, didn't doubt that my face reflected the vehemence I felt. Silence reigned as I stared at her before I finally said, "So what did I say?"

"You said that I am under your protection and the protection of Clan Petran. That no one will ever hurt me."

I nodded approvingly. "And know this: I always keep my word. If he touches you, even looks at you wrong, he will pay with his life."

After a few tense moments, she nodded and then looked out the window. "We're here," she said.

Fawn

I DIDN'T RECOGNIZE THE huge gated house we drove up to, but I knew what awaited me inside. There were several limos gathered in the circular driveway and twice as many menacing figures milling around, some with small machine guns. It could have been a gathering of senators, business leaders. Some of them, especially David, liked to think of themselves as such. But it was a facade, beautifully crafted but fake. The danger and misery beneath that facade was not.

As we exited the limo, I tried to calm my pounding heart and prayed David wouldn't be here, though I knew without a doubt that he would. I also tried to choke back the desire to grab Vasile and hide behind him, beg him to take me away.

Instead, I settled on admiring him. His suit fit perfectly, the jacket cut to show the breadth of his shoulders, his trim waist, the light gray color a perfect complement to the brown of his hair and iciness of his eyes.

It was so different than his usual attire, though I couldn't say better. There was something honest about the way he usually dressed. It told me he didn't pretend, that he knew what and who he was and didn't need to hide behind clothes. It was impressive, a quality I had rarely seen. One I deeply admired.

A spark of desire flared in my stomach as I reflected on that, watched him move with ease and grace and comfort as if he had no question about his place in the world. As annoyed as I'd been, as nervous as I'd been, as nervous as I still was, the attraction toward him, the desire that, as insane as it was, he always stoked in my body hit me like a sledgehammer, made me wish we were anywhere but here, but not to avoid the situation. So I could be with him, feel his strong, powerful body above me again, inside me again.

He glanced at me, and I looked away quickly, feeling a deep flush of embarrassment, though I had no way of knowing if he could tell the direction of my thoughts. I faintly heard the *click* of heels and turned toward the sound and met Natasha's gaze. Her little knowing smile told me she was well aware of what I was thinking, and I couldn't help but grin at her.

That little interlude having relieved some of the tension that had twisted in my stomach, I sped up to stand next to Vasile, feeling almost confident.

"Welcome, Mr. Petran," a tall, thin Hispanic man said in greeting when we reached the double front doors.

"Vargas." Vasile gave the faintest nod but did not lift his hand. The other man didn't seem deterred, and instead waved his extended hand to welcome us in. Fortunately, he didn't even glance in my direction.

We entered a grand entryway with an enormous crystal chandelier and then continued to a large dining room that held a sixteen-seat table, one that was filled by women like me, each more beautiful than the last, showpieces for the array of dangerous-looking men they accompanied.

But all of them, even Vasile, Natasha, and Sorin seemed to disappear when I met David's eyes. He smiled brightly, looking almost like the charming man that had initially won me over. But there was retribution in his gaze, a promise of payback for the embarrassment he'd experienced, though none of it was my fault. It seldom had been, but that had never insulated me from punishment and wouldn't in the future.

I flinched ever so slightly when Vasile touched my arm, and for a millisecond, his face turned down in a frown. But he recovered quickly and led me down the long table and sat directly across from David, his eyes never leaving the other man. I sat next to him, trying to remember what Vasile had said, trying to remember David had no power over me anymore.

A warm hand grasped mine, and I looked at Natasha, saw her faint smile of encouragement. It didn't stop my pounding heart, the almost disembodied feeling that my light head created, but I appreciated the effort.

The next hour was excruciating. I didn't meet David's gaze, but I could feel his eyes on me, and the fear that he'd instilled came back automatically. I wasn't close enough for David to touch, but that didn't mean I wasn't unnerved.

And Vasile wasn't helping. He hadn't looked at me, seemed completely disinterested in me, in everyone around him, save Vargas and David. I followed his lead as Sorin and Natasha did, not eating or drinking or speaking, a silent island in the sea of joviality.

The other guests laughed and drank, all acting as if everything was well, but the undercurrent of tension in the room was unmistakable, and it soon reached the breaking point.

"My food not good enough for you, Mr. Petran?" Vargas finally said.

He sounded friendly, like this was jocular teasing, but the lowering volume in the room, the sudden ratcheting of the tension made the seriousness of the question undeniable.

"We aren't hungry," Vasile said.

Which wasn't a complete lie, at least not for me. I couldn't have eaten a thing, even if forced.

"Fair enough. But you, your brother, your guests," he let his eyes linger on me momentarily before looking at the bar at the opposite side of the room, "drink with me."

"That's a great idea, Vargas," David said, his eyes glued to me. And with each word he spoke a fresh dose of ice and terror raced through my veins. "Offer Mr. Vargas's guests a drink, bitch," he said, mirroring the words that had started this all.

I went to stand, instinct telling me to comply or face the consequences.

Vasile's hand clamped on my wrist, strong but not punishing, and held me in place.

"Apologize."

The lethal tone of his voice froze me and everyone else in the room. After a moment, still halfway between sitting and standing, I shifted to look at Vasile, saw the rage on his face, the tight set of his jaw, his glacial gaze leaving no question of his anger.

"Your English has gotten a lot better," David said, practically sneering.

"Apologize."

"For what? For calling my—"

Something dangerous flitted across Vasile's

face, and David cut off short. I'd never seen that before, David heeding a warning and some small part of me wished he hadn't, wanted him to give Vasile a reason to mete out the damage I'd never have a chance to. But the other, saner part of me wanted peace, wanted out of this whole situation.

The room was tense, heavy with the weight of the brewing confrontation, and all I wanted to do was run.

"Gentlemen, we're here as friends and business associates. Let's not ruin the evening," Vargas said. "I'm sure David meant no offense, Mr. Petran. So he'd be happy to apologize. Wouldn't you, David?"

David looked like he wanted to spit, but he choked out the words, "I apologize, Mr. Petran."

"You didn't insult me," Vasile said evenly. "Apologize."

Vargas's face showed surprise, and David turned an alarming shade of red as disgust tugged at his features. "You're out of your fucking mind. I'm not apologizing to that—"

"You should watch you're fucking mouth," Sorin interjected, voice equally lethal. "Or better yet, don't. Go ahead, say it. See how Clan Petran handles those who disrespect what's ours."

Sorin put extra emphasis on "ours" and the implication was not missed by David. He exhaled hard, his hands clenched into tight fists on the cream-colored tablecloth. I focused on his meaty fingers, remembered the pain they could inflict. He exhaled again, every eye in the room on him, watching.

"I apologize, Fawn," he said.

Vasile didn't look the least bit placated, and it probably wasn't lost on him that David may as well have insulted me again with the venom and scorn in that "apology." I worried what would happen next.

But after a beat, Vasile stood smoothly, then pulled me the rest of the way up. Natasha and Sorin behind, we left the grand home.

14

Vasile

FAWN WAS OUT OF the limo before it came to a complete stop. After speaking with Oleg, I followed her.

"Dammit!"

Her low-voiced words, agitated, not at all Fawn, hit my ears, the wrongness of them amping my reaction.

I walked faster, the sound of her voice and the cursing both cause for alarm, neither something that I had ever heard from Fawn.

When I entered, I zeroed in on her hopping from foot to foot as she clawed at the zipper of her dress.

"What are you doing, Fawn?"

"Trying to get this stupid fucking dress off,"

she said, again reaching for the zipper.

I walked over to her, putting a hand on her shoulder, and after she finally stood still, I pulled the zipper down. She let out a sigh as the material was opened and then made quick work of discarding it. I let my fingers trail across her smooth shoulders and then tightened my grip, turning her toward me and stood silent until she met my eyes.

"What's the matter?"

That moment with David had been unpleasant but necessary, a reminder to him she was mine, a reminder to the others that my word was not to be questioned, and perhaps most importantly, that I wouldn't see her insulted.

"What's the matter is I hate this fucking dress. I hate it! I hate all of it!" she said, voice going venomous. "Being on display, trussed up like a prize turkey to be gawked at, ordered around, a chew toy to be haggled over with no say in the matter."

Her eyes flashed angrily, the slight flare of her nostrils only underscoring her rage. I hadn't intended that, but I also hadn't considered how any of this would look from her perspective, but I could see it clearly now. A rare stab of guilt passed through my heart.

"I..."

"What?" she said, her eyes bugging slightly, pain now glittering in them.

"I just wanted to show him," I finally said, trying to explain, hoping she'd understand.

"Show him what? That ownership has been

transferred? That I'm yours now and not his?"

"Show him that he had no power over you, that no one owns you, not even me," I said quietly.

Her lip trembled and tears began streaming down her face. I stroked my thumb across her cheek to gather her tears, then leaned forward and pressed my lips against hers.

Fawn

I DIDN'T KNOW WHAT I had expected, wasn't sure what had made me think he wouldn't care how I felt, think that he wouldn't react, but whatever I had expected, it hadn't been this. Anger. Yes. Coldness. Distance. All were possibilities. But this gentleness, almost sweetness, hadn't even crossed my mind.

It shoved me off balance and made me want him even more.

I exhaled and let myself revel in his touch. Vasile's kiss was different, no less potent but there was an openness, a kindness, as if he was trying to show me the truth of his words through his touch. But he didn't push or deepen the kiss. Instead he held back, silently urging me to take the lead.

It was more than anyone had ever offered, and something I wanted to take. I pressed my lips against his harder, slipped my tongue between them as I curled my fingers in the hair at the base of his neck. He put his hands on my hips, his body coiled with restrained power, but he didn't press and that restraint made me want him all the more.

So I kissed him freely, with abandon, let my hands touch him. I let my hands move over his always-rough jaw, down the fine, expensive-feeling cotton of his shirt, down his hard chest. Without breaking our connection, I opened the two buttons that held his jacket together and laid my hands flat against his hard stomach and chest. Even through his shirt, I felt the heat of his skin and wanted more.

Vasile kept his hands on my hips, and though he tightened them, pushed his lips against mine, he didn't try to take over. I pulled his shirt from his pants, and the soft *whish* of fabric sounded low in the room, only heightening the already throbbing need that had overtaken me. I finally broke the kiss and looked up at him, his eyes dark, lids heavy.

I walked my fingers up his chest and then pulled at the knot of his tie, yanking it off him. He'd been devastating in his suit, but I wanted him, the real him, and I made haste to remove the fine clothes that hid the man underneath. I worked his buttons open one by one, excitement heightening at each scrap of ink-covered skin that was exposed. And after I'd pushed the shirt off his shoulders I stared at him, the heavy slabs of his chest, his tight stomach, the hard ridge that tented his pants.

One breath, then another, and I pressed my body against his, my breasts against his chest and then pressed my hand against that ridge as I kissed the smooth, hot skin that covered his collarbone. He exhaled quickly and then ran his hands up my back, the slight roughness of his hands against my skin setting off sizzling embers of desire that settled at the apex of my thighs. I kept my hand pressed against him and then worked open his belt and quickly lowered his pants.

His iron-hard cock was damp with his desire, but he didn't try to hasten me, not even when I gripped him, huffing out at the touch of the velvet-soft skin of his shaft and not even when he shuddered after I circled the mushroom-shaped head of his cock. He gripped my hip tight, exhaled, but stayed still as I stroked him, wanting to feel every vein, every millimeter of his soft skin, feel his hardness pulse in my palm.

Then I released him and pushed him down on the edge of the bed. He leaned back on his hands, his huge chest heaving, his cock rising from between his legs, beckoning me.

I answered the call and stepped toward him and then straddled him slowly. I reached between our bodies and gripped the base of his shaft, stroked it along my slit. We both cried out at the contact, and Vasile again grabbed my hip, his hold almost punishing, but the gleam of pleasure in his eye more than worth it. I circled my clit with the head of his cock and then lifted my hips and centered him at the edge of my opening.

Gazes connected, I lowered slowly, filling myself with him inch by inch until he was fully inside me, our bodies as close as they could possibly be. I wrapped my legs around him, and then he sat up, put his arms around me, crushing my breasts against his chest. I was surrounded by him, couldn't break away unless he allowed. But here, like this, was as safe, as loved as I had ever felt.

He bit at my shoulder, and I pressed my lips against his neck and then, wrapped in his embrace, I rocked against him in an awkward rhythm that was absolutely perfect. My breathing grew erratic as the pleasure swelled and Vasile's hardness pulsed inside me, his warm breath on my shoulder, his arms around my back showing me his pleasure better than anything else could.

Then he stilled, went rigid beneath me, and the first jet of his cum triggered my own release.

15

Vasile

"VARGAS SEND YOU?" I asked Priest without bothering to look up.

"No one sends me anywhere," he replied before he settled across from me at the table.

"So to what do I owe this visit?" I asked, leaning back to look at him.

He just shook his head. "That was foolish, Vasile."

"So I should have let that idiot insult me? Insult her?" I said, slamming my hand on the table.

"And what of Vargas? You were in his home," Priest said.

"I'll give him back five percent. That should soothe any hard feelings," I said.

"It will," Priest said. "So have you considered expanding relations with Clan Constantin?"

"So the lecture is over?"

"How many times have I told you I wouldn't waste my breath on a Petran?" he said.

Fawn

"I WAIT OUTSIDE," OLEG said, his words slow, heavy with his accent.

He stood at the front door shuffling nervously and not meeting my eyes.

"Yes. I don't need anything," I said carefully in deference to the language barrier, nodding and smiling, though both were probably lost on him since he hadn't actually looked at me directly.

"You stay here?" he said, meeting my eyes this time, face serious.

"Yes." I ended with another smile and after a moment, he turned to leave.

Vasile had left before dawn this morning, told me that Oleg would be here to watch me. I hadn't liked the sound of that, had had half a mind to protest, but habit made me hold my tongue. Now that I was alone, the silence was disquieting.

Somehow, in just these few days, he'd filled my world, the tension and uncertainty of our first meeting and then later, the intensity of our coupling had filled my mind. And now that he was gone, thoughts I'd fought hard to keep at bay were rearing their heads, thoughts of one person in particular.

Esther.

I'd never told anyone about her, hadn't had anyone to tell. And I forced myself not to think about her because thinking about her meant I had to think about myself, think about the life I had let David take from me.

It hurt.

Badly.

But last night, held in the cocoon of safety that Vasile's arms had become, feeling a peace that had always evaded me, I'd opened that door. And now, even though he wasn't here, the door remained open.

I jumped up from my perch, grabbed my handbag, and was headed toward the front door before I stopped to think.

Back then, Esther had lived about twelve blocks from here. Maybe she still did. I had nothing but time so I could go and see.

I reached for the doorknob and looked at the car, Oleg sitting inside. I debated whether or not to get his attention. It seemed wise, but he'd want to come with me, and the lure of exploring, maybe finding something of myself by myself was too alluring of a pull.

So I stood, torn. Then I shook my head and opened the door. Vasile had said I wasn't a prisoner, that I belonged to no one but myself, so I needed to start acting like I wasn't.

My heart thudded as I walked away, a voice at the back of my head nagging at me that I was doing something wrong, that I would get in trouble.

And it was that very thought that pushed me on.

Trouble.

I didn't belong to anyone, didn't answer to anyone. And I was sick and tired of feeling like I had to.

Anger at the very thought of being in trouble carried me through the first half of my journey, but as the anger faded, worry sprang up in its place.

What if she'd moved?

What if she didn't remember me?

What if she didn't care anymore?

That thought was most chilling of all. She had no reason to care. I'd dropped out of her life, tossed away a lifelong friendship because of him. I could try to explain, hope she understood I had stayed away to protect her, but I was doubtful and even worse, I couldn't blame her.

And then I cursed myself for being so self-absorbed. It had been years since I'd been like this, unaccompanied, free to look at whatever I wanted without fear, and instead of focusing on the world around me, I was stuck in my head, still letting others control me.

But no more.

I slowed, looked around, allowing myself to stare, letting my gaze linger as I remembered different places I had visited before my night-mare had begun.

And as I walked, a sense of weightlessness, of possibility came over me.

It was far too short-lived.

I caught a movement out of the corner of my eye, and when I looked up, there David stood.

I couldn't believe I'd gotten this close to him without even noticing it, but now that I had, every fiber of my being was on alert. He still wore that awful cologne, and I wrinkled my nose involuntarily, seemingly having again fallen out of the habit of schooling my emotions in front of him.

He was impeccably dressed as always, but I noticed the redness of his eyes, the puffy bags underneath them. He wasn't sleeping, which always made him more volatile than usual...

I mentally shook myself. I didn't have to anticipate anymore, try to predict what would confront me at any given moment. I didn't have to be around him at all. That thought made me look harder, deeper, not glance at him with hooded eyes, trying to see without being noticed, but really look at him.

And when my eyes clashed with his, I saw pleading there, and the simmering anger that never seemed to go away.

I turned abruptly, determined to get far away from him as fast as I could.

"Stop!" he yelled.

And I almost did.

Almost.

But Vasile's voice floated through my mind, reminded me that I didn't have to obey.

I kept walking.

"Fawn!" David called, sounding almost desperate. "You need to come home now. Come home!"

I didn't turn, but I heard the urgency in his raw voice. David was desperate. Was pleading, seemed almost hurt.

Good. Let him hurt.

I added a little spring to my step.

16

Fawn

I TURNED THE CORNER and walked down a tidy block, memories of the years Esther and I had spent here taking over. Everything was almost the same, so much so that I could picture the little girl I'd been, so hopeful, so anxious to start life. I missed that little girl, but I knew that she was gone forever, and I needed to find the woman who would take her place. Doing this would be the first step.

I walked up the small porch and knocked.

As I waited, listening to the person inside moving around, it hit me that it was nine in the morning, right around the time when most people would be headed to work, after that even.

The door opened.

"Fawn?"

Esther looked at me with question in her eyes and then stood silent.

I furrowed my brow, stared up at her, her round, deceptively angelic face a mask of confusion.

"Hi, Esther. I—"

My words were cut off by the tight embrace that she pulled me into. She crushed me against her, holding me as if she never wanted to let me go. And I held her back, tears flowing from my eyes.

"You were going somewhere?" I asked after a long moment.

"Nowhere important," she said as she pulled back a fraction of an inch to look at me, not smiling but the joy in her eyes unmistakable. "Come in," she said.

Fawn

THE HOURS HAD SLID by like minutes, us talking about nothing and everything, the easy camaraderie we'd found in first grade coming back as if it had never been gone.

"You remember Mr. Richards, don't you? How you were my little accomplice?" she said suddenly, turning her head toward me.

She lay with her back on the floor, ridiculously long legs splayed on the couch, the position one she'd favored since childhood.

"Grams is going to beat your butt if she catches you like that, Esther."

For the first time in hours, her smile dropped. "Yeah, she would have." Esther sighed and then sat up, swinging her legs to the floor and then propping against the couch. "She passed about six years ago now."

"I hadn't heard..."

Esther nodded. "I know." Then she smiled. "She always said she knew you'd come back one day. I'm glad you're here, Fawn."

I nodded and then tried to lift the solemn moment.

"You know, I always paid for it," I said, remembering how she'd get me to distract the old man so she could steal candy.

"You did not!" she exclaimed.

"I did. It was the only reason I went along. Why'd you do it, anyway?"

"I had a reputation to maintain then," she said with a shrug. "It was stupid too because if Grams had ever suspected me of stealing..."

She shivered at the thought, and then Esther lifted one corner of her mouth. "Do you think Mr. Richards was in on it? I mean, stealth has never been my strong suit, but he never seemed to notice," she said.

"He was," I replied with a smile.

She just shook her head. "I blame you for all the years I wasted dreaming I'd be a cat burglar."

Then she bounded up and used her long

strides to go to the credenza.

"Look, Fawn!" She returned and shoved a picture into my hand.

I stared at it and then looked back at Esther. "Is that James?"

"I know, right? Little rug rat is in the Coast Guard now."

"I can't..." I started but then trailed off. James had been a pesky kid desperate to go wherever his cool older sister did, and now he was grown up. And I'd missed it. Hadn't been there for any of the big moments in my best friend's life.

Esther grabbed my hand and squeezed it tight.

"Don't do that. What matters now is that you're away from him, that you're here." And then her stomach rumbled loudly. "Sorry to interrupt this touching moment," she said.

I laughed and then my eyes met hers.

"Enzo's?" we said simultaneously.

An hour later, stuffed with the city's best pizza and slightly buzzed on the white wine Esther had pulled out, we both lay on the living room floor, another scene that had played out countless times before.

"You still getting fired from every job you ever had?" I asked.

"Nope. I quit sometimes now too," Esther replied.

"One day..."

"I'll be employable? Maybe. But I tell them all the time if they'd just do things the way I say, we wouldn't have any problems," she said, her booming voice filling the room.

"I don't think it works that way, Esther."

"It should," she said flatly.

I laughed out loud again, and then we went quiet, looking through the big picture window as night fell.

"I'm glad you're here, Fawn," she said again, this time serene.

"Me too."

"I'm glad you got away from him."

"Me too."

"You could have come here. Anytime."

"I know."

"And you're done now. Forever. Out of that world?"

I stayed silent, not sure what to say. And then I began. "I—"

A pounding at the door cut my words off.

17

Vasile

I STOOD ON THE porch of the small, tidy house, but I hardly saw it or the neighborhood it sat in. The concern chased by rage left me incapable of noticing much, and I wouldn't be able to until I saw her. That she had been so close when I'd spent hours searching for her far and wide only added to the anger.

"May I help you?" the tall, voluptuous black woman who answered the door asked.

I gazed at her for a moment and then pushed past her to enter. She stepped in front of me, silently daring me to try to come farther, no hint of fear in her face. On one hand, it pleased me that Fawn had someone who cared for her so deeply she'd put her own safety at risk. But on the other...

My patience was frayed to the point of snapping, the unfamiliar worry that had taken over when Fawn was nowhere to be found having taxed my reserves.

"Fawn," I said, not taking my eyes away from the woman.

Her scowl dropped ever so slightly and I could see the pulse at the base of her neck speed, but she stood her ground.

"There's no one here by that name. Now you need to leave before I call the cops," the woman said sternly, arms crossed over her ample chest.

"Esther, it's okay."

Esther looked to Fawn and then to me, lingering on my tattoos and then meeting my eyes. She didn't even make an effort to hide her scorn, but I didn't care. Seeing Fawn had loosened the ball of tension that had taken residence in my gut.

And replaced it with a seething anger at her carelessness that almost made my hands shake. "Let's go." I practically growled the words, and Esther narrowed her eyes and then gulped nervously.

Fawn stood still, seeming to make no effort to move, so I sidestepped Esther and went to Fawn, searching her eyes for some explanation. I saw none, but I would get my answer.

"Vasile, what—"

She stopped short when I lifted her off her feet and turned to leave.

"Wait! You can't do that!" Esther yelled, walking behind us, pulling hard at my arms to try and release Fawn.

I stopped and turned to look at her. "I wouldn't do that if I were you," I said quietly, hoping the woman understood that I was serious.

She stood still, mouth dropped open with surprise but eyes burning fire.

"It's okay, Esther. I'm fine," Fawn said.

Her current position, held so tight against my chest she could barely move, probably didn't give the other woman comfort, but I didn't care. What mattered was that even in the face of my anger, she wasn't afraid.

"You don't have to, Fawn. Not this time," the other woman said, voice both pleading and emphatic.

"I'll call you," Fawn said as I walked out of the door with her still crushed against my chest.

18

Fawn

HE HADN'T EVEN LOOKED at me once he'd put me in the car, and the waves of rage that rolled off him made me shiver, made me wonder if maybe I'd pushed too far.

"Vasile, I—"

"Say nothing!"

His thundering voice filled with malice I had never heard from him, at least not directed at me, boomed through the car and right down to my soul. But instead of fear, his voice, icy cold and distant, sparked anger. I stayed silent, but not because he was as angry as I'd ever seen him. I stayed silent because I didn't trust myself to have a reasonable conversation with him, not when he was like this.

So we rode back to the house, the car tense and silent, and before I could get out, he had again scooped me up and held me in a tight grip.

"I'm capable of walking you know," I said snidely, unable to hold my tongue.

"Maybe, eh? It seems simple but you've proven today I can't trust you with simple things."

"What does—"

He turned his icy-green glare at me, and I went silent, though I still seethed with anger. We entered the house and he tossed me directly on the bed.

"If you think—"

My words were yet again cut off, but this time by his hard, insistent kiss. He conquered my mouth, not giving me any quarter, space to talk, think, barely even to breathe. He kissed me thoroughly, tongue stroking every inch of my mouth. But it wasn't a kiss of passion. There was possession as there had always been, but something deeper, the way he kissed me, touched me almost like he needed to make sure I was really there.

I sighed into his mouth, opening to him, and he took advantage, mastering my mouth with his tongue, my body with his hands. No part of me went untouched as he moved his hands over me as if relearning the feel of my body.

And then he was gone. His hand fell away from my body, his mouth released mine, and he stared at me, eyes still icy but now deep with something else.

Two quick movements, and he'd removed the button-down shirt from my body, and in another, he'd discarded the pale pink bra underneath. I watched him as he watched me, gaze moving over the rounds of my breasts, the puckered buds of my nipples. I wanted to arch, lean forward in offering, but something in his eyes held me still. And though my mind raced with images of him touching me, he did not, but instead, pulled my pants and panties down and off my body and cast them and my shoes aside.

He'd seen me like this before, but I felt more vulnerable now, couldn't tell what he was thinking, especially not when he stood and discarded his own clothing.

His cock, thick and hard, jutted out from the nest of darkish brown hair, and as it always seemed to, my throat went dry. And this time, I couldn't stop the little squirm-shiver that rushed over my body, the anticipation of having him inside me too great to bear.

As he moved toward me, his cock bobbed, hitting his stomach, and even in the dim light of the bedroom, I could see the slick arousal that had gathered at the head, the other drops that leaked from him freely.

On instinct, I lay back, and he climbed atop me, his cock finding my core unerringly. He pushed in and filled me with one solid stroke. He hadn't bothered with preparation, and I was so full, I worried I couldn't hold him, felt the sharp sting of unprepared flesh stretching around his girth.

That sting intensified and then melted into a pleasure-pain that froze my lungs when he moved. He thrust inside me hard, unrelenting, not kissing or touching me as he had before. And through it all, he held my gaze, his eyes stone cold, unreadable, his face a mask of anger.

Before I could stop myself, I reached for him, tangled my fingers in his hair, and I thought I saw a shift in his expression, some sign of the softness I had seen glimpses of before.

But in a flash it was gone, and he hooded his eyes and thrust harder.

I squeaked out a moan and then held his huge shoulders, deciding, at least for now, to focus on the pleasure he was giving me. He'd never felt quite so distant, not even when we were so new to each other, but my body couldn't tell the difference, and as he moved, pleasure coursed through me. When he stroked even harder, burying himself inside me so deep his pelvis pressed my clit, I exploded in climax, my eyes slamming shut against the orgasm he had ripped from me.

He went still above me, his cock throbbing inside me as he spent himself, the warm burst of his seed painting my womb.

Before my breath had slowed, he pulled away, my body feeling empty without his hardness, my arms equally empty without his body.

He stood, his softening cock, now wet with our juices, still impressive. Then he looked down at me again with Arctic eyes.

"Don't ever do something so stupid again,"

he said, and then he turned.

The remnants of pleasure dissipated in the face of his disdain, at the sharpness and censure in his tone, and I sat up.

"Something stupid like what, leave the house unattended? Go visit a friend? You said I wasn't a prisoner here. Was that a lie?" I said, voice low in my throat.

He stopped and stood still, the broad expanse of his tattoo-covered back and his powerful legs making him menacing, an effect that only intensified when he turned back to face me.

"No, you're not a prisoner, but you don't understand. It's not safe..." he said, his voice going low on the last word.

I thought of David, of the other enemies Vasile no doubt had, and realization clicked in my mind. "You were worried?"

He didn't agree, but he didn't deny my words either, which was answer enough. I stood, uncaring of my nudity or the trickle of cum that ran down my leg.

"I was careful. I know—"

"You don't know anything," he said coldly.

"What? Nothing like how that," I pointed at the tattoo on his left shoulder, "means you're fourth-generation clan. Or how that one," I pointed right below his ribs, "made you and tells the story of your first murder. Or how that one," I put my hand over his left pec, "means you can be trusted and will never snitch." I grabbed his hands and ran my fingers across his knuckles. "Or how each of these tells the story of a clan war you fought in."

"How do...?" he asked.

"I was there for years, Vasile. Saw everything. I know all about the Peruvians, the other clans, the Sicilians, and David who washes all of your dirty money, his father who did so before him," I said.

"Fawn..."

"What? I told you I wasn't stupid. I know what you are. I know what you do. And I know the risks. I just needed to see her. I owed her that much, wanted it for myself. Needed to do it alone," I said.

He grabbed me and pulled me into an air-stealing embrace. "Fine, but don't ever leave like that. I didn't know where you were, and I thought—"

"Now! Take me to her now, or I'm burning this bitch down!"

I pulled away and looked at Vasile, whose surprised expression probably mirrored my own, and then we both looked toward the closed door.

"Looks like Esther's here," I said.

Fawn

AFTER HASTILY DRESSING, I followed Vasile out the door to stand in the drive where Esther stood, Oleg behind her looking like he didn't know what to do, Sorin in front of her, his face a mix of danger and slightly unhinged humor.

"I don't care who you are, I want to see her now, or I'll—"

"You'll what, huh? Call the cops?" Sorin said, his voice that mix of laughter and lethal I had come to know was uniquely his.

Esther's eyes flashed with fire, and she stood toe to toe with Sorin, his height making her look up, something I knew was novel for her. And though her eyes flashed, she wasn't uncontrolled, not in the least. Instead, she seemed coolly detached, determined, uncaring that Sorin stared down at her with malice.

I moved quickly to intercede, worried about what Vasile might do, but at that moment more interested in putting distance between Esther and Sorin.

Sorin turned his eyes toward me, twisted his face in that easy smile that made my heart beat a little faster, but with worry not affection. "Can you believe this, Vasile? This *scroafă* has some nerve, eh?"

"You ain't seen nothing yet. This 'screwfa' is about to—"

"Esther! What are you doing here?"

At the sound of my voice, Esther tossed Sorin another dirty look and then ran to me.

"Jesus fucking Christ, Fawn! I thought that guy..."

She trailed off, the worry on her face, her furrowed brow telling me exactly what she'd thought.

"How did you find me?"

"Wasn't too difficult. Fucking cops pointed me right to the door. Said it was my funeral if I dared come here. Pussies."

Sorin laughed, but then quickly went quiet.

"And my guards? How did you get past them?" Vasile asked.

Esther looked at him briefly, then shrugged. "Wasn't too hard. I just waited until they weren't looking."

Vasile's face dropped as did my heart at the thought of what might have happened if she'd been intercepted.

"Esther, that was dangerous. You shouldn't have..."

"I didn't once, Fawn." She shook her head emphatically. "Never again."

Her brow was still furrowed with worry, but her lips were pursed and set into a stubborn line, and I could see her determination and her concern.

"I'm fine, Esther."

She squeezed my hand and then looked first at Vasile, who stood silent, an indulgence I'd have to thank him for later, and then at Sorin scornfully.

"You sure?" she tossed out, not moving her eyes from Sorin.

"Yes," I said.

She didn't look convinced.

∭

Vasile

SORIN STARED AT THE woman, and I could see the calculation in his brain. Fawn would be fine with her. Sorin, on the other hand, who knew how he would react?

"Come, Sorin. Let the women talk." I headed toward the car, and Sorin looked as if he would protest but then followed behind me.

"Who the fuck is that? And how did she get here? And what makes her think we'll tolerate her sticking her nose in where it doesn't belong?" he asked.

"She was determined," I said. "But that's no excuse. I'll need to talk to Oleg. I don't like the idea of anyone getting this close so easily."

"I like to talk. I'll handle it," he said with a grim little smile.

"Just to talk, Sorin. She's harmless."

"I doubt it. She was about to take a swing at me."

"You probably deserved it. She looks tough. Do you think you could have handled her?" I asked.

"Asshole," Sorin said playfully.

"So where was Fawn? With that woman?" he asked.

I nodded. I'd had Sorin and some of the others quietly searching for her during the day.

"She can't be doing that, Vasile."

Sorin was completely serious now, which only reinforced how bad those hours without her had been, how she needed to understand she could never do that again.

"We discussed it," I said, my words calm and casual and in no way a reflection of how I felt.

Sorin looked skeptical. "Discussed it? That's it?"

"Should I beat her to prove my point?" I wouldn't, not ever, but many others didn't share my reserve.

"Father would have."

"Good thing I'm not Father then," I said.

Sorin frowned, but I could see the war in his mind. We'd loved our father, admired him, but there were things that he'd done to our mother that I wouldn't be able to forgive, forget, and would never emulate. It was up to Sorin to decide whether he would do the same.

"I'm moving back to the house," I said.

"You love her," Sorin said.

"No, but she needs space, and I need to keep a better eye on her," I said.

Sorin smiled, this time genuinely, no trace of anger at all. "Of course, brother."

Fawn

ESTHER FROWNED AT ME and then shook her head.

"What did you expect me to do, Fawn?"

"Not come here," I said, still boggled at what she had done, what she'd risked.

"Right. I'm supposed to let that menacing-as-fuck dude walk into my home, bodily remove my best friend from it, and not do a thing?"

"He's a good man," I said. "He would never hurt me." And I knew he wouldn't, trusted that knowledge in a way that I had trusted little else in my life.

Esther stayed silent, her lips puckered into a tight grimace, and I knew what she was thinking before she even said it. "I'm smarter now. He is...what he is. But I'm safer with him than I've ever been with anyone else."

She looked unconvinced. "Come stay with me. Try something different," Esther said, eyes imploring.

I didn't entertain the thought, not even for a moment. Couldn't entertain the thought of not being with him.

"I'm where I belong. With whom I belong."

And I knew it to be true. It didn't make sense, but it didn't have to. I was where I wanted to be. I could see Esther struggle, knew that she wanted to argue, to try to persuade me. The girl I'd known all those years ago wouldn't have held her tongue. But she did. And that made me wonder what other changes I'd missed. I planned to find out.

"One phone call, that's all it will take, Fawn," she said, pulling herself to her full height and crossing her arms over her chest.

"You're gonna come in commando-style, rescue me?"

"More like nag-or-insult-the-big-scary-men-until-they-give-me-what-I-want style, but you get the idea," she responded.

I laughed. "I appreciate it, but I'm not a damsel in distress. I don't need anyone to rescue me. But I want you back in my life. I miss my best friend," I said.

If I didn't know better, I would have thought there was a tear in my friend's eye, but if so, she recovered quickly and flashed me a bright smile.

"You won't be able to get rid of me," she said.

"I didn't think so, but I'll make sure to keep you away from Sorin," I said.

"Who? The dude at the door?" she asked incredulously.

"Yeah. The huge, kind of crazy Romanian dude you were barking at. You're nuts, standing up to him like that."

"I'm perfectly sane, and I was confident I could handle him if necessary," Esther said, voice brimming with unshakable confidence. "But in the spirit of reunification, let's hope it doesn't come to that. You gonna drop by this weekend?"

"I'd love to," I said.

19

Vasile

Two Months Later

"ARE WE DONE HERE?" I asked.

Priest nodded, and I stood, ready to leave.

"You aren't hanging out tonight?" Sorin said.

I shook my head, and he frowned. "Going to play house? Again."

"Careful, brother," I said, letting a warning edge bleed into my voice.

"Suit yourself," he replied, and then he turned and headed behind the closed doors to Priest's inner sanctum.

I left without looking back, but while my steps carried sure and true to my destination, my mind urged me to slow down. Not that I paid it any attention or could have stopped myself even if I had. The urgent, clawing need I felt whenever I was away from Fawn ripped at me, and I knew it wouldn't subside until I saw her again, held her body against mine so close that nothing else mattered.

She did that to me, made me think and feel things I hadn't ever, made me more than clan and at the same time less. Made me a man, one who had become addicted to a woman. This ruse would have to stop at some point. She'd want her life, a chance to be away from me, away from memories of the monster I'd taken her from.

But until then, when she finally came to her senses, I'd take as much of her as I could.

I'd gotten her settled at my father's estate. He'd acquired it from a prominent family that owed him, and he'd been so proud of it, the huge house and exclusive address proof to himself that he'd finally made it. He hadn't enjoyed it long though, dying less than two years after he'd gotten it. But in just weeks, Fawn had managed to make it feel like a home.

Our home.

When I arrived and entered, I heard her in the kitchen, and as I came to her, she smiled at me, her eyes going soft. "Vasile, I..."

I cut her off with a hard kiss, covering her lips with mine and then swooping my tongue inside her mouth. I kissed her with everything I had, trying to give physical form to emotions I couldn't name, feelings that went beyond words.

And when I pulled back and stared down at her, her lips wet and swollen from my kisses, her brown eyes wide and lit with that unrestrained passion I could never get enough of, I lost control.

Hands on her shoulders, I turned her so that she was face-first against the kitchen island. "Oh!" she said when I lifted the long T-shirt she wore and revealed the smooth expanse of her back and the plush curves of her ass, the thin little scrap of her thong peeking from between her cheeks.

"Did you wear this for me?" I asked as I hooked one finger, then another under the string.

I got closer and exhaled, watching as goose bumps rose across her skin. I kissed the padded point of her shoulder blade and then chuckled low when a full-body shiver thrashed through her.

"Did you, Fawn?" I asked as I pulled the panties down her thighs.

She opened automatically and I lowered them until they dropped around her ankles.

"Y-yes," she said quietly, her voice breaking as I stroked my fingers over her full hip and then over her thigh.

"Nice," I said, but that didn't get to half the matter. She'd told me how much she disliked being on display, so that she'd worn such a garment for me sent my desire sparking and my heart seizing with a feeling I didn't yet dare give name to.

"Vasile..." she said on a broken moan when I traced her smooth mound and then went lower to delve between her slick, plump lips.

"What?" I whispered as I lazily stroked a finger against her soft skin, my already titanium-hard dick firming even more at the wetness that greeted my finger.

"Someone might see," she said.

"Then let them see," I said. "Would you like that, knowing they are watching me fuck you, knowing they are jealous because they can't have you, will never taste your sweet pussy, feel you clamping around them?"

"Umm..." she mumbled.

The words were unintelligible, but her body told the tale. Her clit was hard and throbbing against my fingers, her sex wet and getting wetter every second.

As I toyed with her, I fumbled with my belt, anxious to again feel her around me, to finally be at peace. My cock sprang free when I lowered my pants, practically straining toward her, already slick with precum. She reached back, but before she touched me, I grabbed her arm.

"No," I said sharply, punctuating the statement with a quick little slap to her ass.

She moaned low in her throat and arched back toward me, seeking more. I almost came on the spot, the sight of Fawn's face twisted in pleasure, her eyes shut tight, sparking another burst of warmth in my chest.

"Hands in front," I said and without hesitation, she complied. "Good."

And then I went quiet, kissing my way down the skin of her back, the little tremors that racked through her making me smile.

"Ahh," she moaned out when I reached the curve of her hip.

I went lower, kissing and licking the little indentation at the base of her spine. Then lower, tracing her crevice between her full cheeks. I stopped when I reached her rosette and swirled the tight hole. Fawn went rigid, and I glanced up, feeling a deep sense of pride when I saw how tightly she gripped the countertop, the edges of her knuckles turning white with the strength of her hold.

Swipe after swipe, I licked at her hole and then pushed my tongue in, spreading her open bit by bit. And as I worked at her back hole with my tongue, I worked her front with my fingers, plucking at her clit and then dipping into her cunt. The low, guttural cries that spilled from her throat emboldened me, and I increased my pace, licking and stroking her with an urgency that made my movements jerky.

"Please..." she said on a low moan when I pulled away.

I breathed deep, heart thundering, my chest rising and falling with heavy breaths, my cock hard enough to hammer steel. Squared behind her, I closed the distance between our bodies and pushed my rod between her lips, moaning myself at the first touch of her petal-soft skin against my shaft.

"Please what, Fawn?" I whispered, the volume of my voice completely at odds with the need that rode at me. "You want me to fuck you?" I asked, pushing against her, the friction setting off a wave of pleasure that tugged at my gut.

"Yes," she said.

"Yes, what?" I asked, holding still though every fiber of my being demanded I slam into her.

"Please fuck me," she said.

"Where? Here?" I grabbed the base of my cock and ran my cockhead along her lips before I used it to spread them and pushed up until I was barely breaching her entry. "Or here?"

I thrust against her until my cock was coated with her cream and then pulled back and aimed at her back hole. She stood straighter, and the movement pulled me inside her just a few centimeters, but enough I could feel the hot heat of her tunnel, the delicate pulse of her hole as she closed around me.

My heart stuttered, and I grabbed her generous hip, needing something to hold.

"Wherever you want," she said. "I'm yours."

Before the words had fully fallen from her lips, I thrust gently, giving her a tiny bit more before I met resistance. The angel on my shoulder told me to stop, reminded me Fawn was gentle, wasn't ready for this, that she probably never would be.

But the devil on the other shoulder, the

one that wanted to possess all of her, demanded I take her, bury my cock as deep inside her as it would go.

That angel had made few appearances in my life, had been listened to even less, and I didn't plan to change that tonight.

I thrust harder this time, groaning when her tight passage gave way. Both of my hands were anchored on her waist, my hold so strong that some faint part of me wondered if I'd leave bruises. But I couldn't loosen my grip, too afraid the urge to slam into her would take over.

So I held her tight and filled her slowly, inch by inch, until I was balls-deep inside her.

"Fawn…" I trailed off and slammed my eyes shut, hardly able to think let alone speak when I was deep inside her, her channel pulsing around me. She shifted experimentally, and I bucked in response, the reverberation of pleasure making me grip her even tighter.

"Move. Please move," she cried, voice low.

"Anything for you," I bit out through gritted teeth, rocking against her with slow, shallow strokes, not quite able to believe, but happy beyond belief she was so passionately responding to me taking her this way.

When my fingers found her clit and I strummed at the hard bud, she jerked around me, and that little movement broke the dam. I thrust harder and then harder, all the while playing with her clit. As I continued to pump into her, I moved my hand down and pushed one finger, then another into her pussy, and both of us cried out at the new sensation of my cock filling one hole, my fingers in the other, a thin membrane of tissue the only thing separating the two.

I retreated and returned over and over and over again, my finger in her pussy moving in time with my cock in her ass, her throaty moans mingling with my own, her curvy body trembling beautifully with each stroke, and I again marveled at how perfectly she fit me, how right it felt to have her under me, to be inside her.

And then she clenched down around me, her womb fluttering against my fingers, her ass gripped down tight on my rod. I stilled, held her as she rode out the wave of her orgasm. When she calmed, I began again, moving inside her in hard, deep thrusts that soon had her panting. As I moved, her hole loosened but still held me in a glove-tight hold that made me see stars.

The low churn that had filled my stomach boiled over, and on a final thrust, I stilled and let the pleasure take me, jet after jet of cum pouring out of me and deep inside her. I snaked my arms around her waist and put my head on her back, lying against her soft body as the most intense pleasure—body and soul—I'd ever felt overtook me.

Fawn

THE NEXT MORNING I lay in his—our—ridiculously huge bed. This was one of the rare mornings that he was with me. He was usually gone before I rose and had never slept longer than me in all the nights we'd been together. In fact, I didn't know if I could ever recall him sleeping, but he did so now.

I drank him in greedily, sleep giving the usually harsh shadows of his features a softness that was uncommon.

He looked at peace.

The desire to touch him, push soft hair away from his forehead, trace my fingers along his stubbled jaw almost overcame me. But I resisted, wanted to see him at peace as much as I could.

I didn't have too long though because I could sense the very instant he woke. His eyes popped open, slightly soft from sleep but completely alert, and his gaze swept to mine.

Then he looked down to my nipples, which pebbled at his first glance. And for once, the desire to hide wasn't there. Only the desire to have him see me. His gaze swept lower, but when it landed on my hips, his eyes went cold, hard with displeasure.

He reached out, sculpted gentle fingertips over the mottled finger marks. His brows flattened and he pulled his lips into a thin line, jaw working from the way he clinched his teeth.

"I hurt you," he said.

I lifted my hand and smoothed the tips of my fingers atop his, touching him as gently as he touched me. He looked up, gaze clashing with mine.

"I like them," I said softly.

He lifted a brow, unspoken question clear.

"They're from you. And not because you hurt me, but because you wanted me. So every time I see them, touch them, I can remember how that felt."

I smiled at him, but his expression didn't change. Instead, he rose up on his elbow and then moved until he loomed over me, the wide breadth of his shoulders blocking the sunlight.

But I wasn't afraid, hadn't really been since that first day. I knew the power of his body, knew the gentleness with which he touched me, knew that he wouldn't hurt me even though he was more than able. And I felt safe with him huge and powerful over me.

He shifted until his hands were on either side of my head, knees between mine.

I wrapped my legs around his waist, and he found my center unerringly, moving inside of me with one solid stroke.

Air expelled from my lungs, and the sensation of having him inside me, all around me, sparked a sense of passion and calm that was as disconcerting and addictive as the man who created it.

His hardness pulsed inside me, and I clamped my walls around him and was rewarded with a sharp intake of breath. I did it again and again, tightening and releasing around his cock as I trailed my fingers across his arms and chest, lingering on the tattoos for a moment before I moved my hands up and swiped my thumb across his strong jaw, the shell of his ear, before I locked my fingers at the base of his neck much as I had wrapped my ankles around his waist.

I kept my gaze on his, begging him without words, hoping that at least for a while he could see what I saw, know that I trusted him completely. My eyes drifted shut when he moved and pushed himself inside me, gentle at first and then with increasing speed and urgency. When his lips covered mine, I opened automatically and he speared his tongue inside my mouth as he speared his cock inside my pussy. I breathed out harsh breaths, but no sound left my mouth, all caught by him the same as I caught his own deep exhales and low-voiced moans.

And when he pulsed a final time and then filled my womb with his seed, I knew I would love him forever.

Later, after we'd drifted off between long, slow kisses and caresses, he turned to me and rested his hand on my shoulder, the idle movements of his calloused fingers against my skin stirring a wave of delicious sensation.

"Last night," he said, his deep, husky voice stirring sensation of its own, "you stayed up for me. Why?"

I looked into his eyes, felt apprehension spark. I'd been intent on talking to him last night, had stayed up, unwilling to wait for fear of losing my nerve, but his passion and then the exhaustion after had robbed me of my will. And now, I had to tell him. But I didn't know how he would react.

"Fawn," he said, expectant, practically daring me not to answer.

"I think... I suspect I'm pregnant."

My lungs were so tight with apprehension, I had barely been able to get the last word out. I trusted him, but Vasile was still a mystery to me, and I had no idea how he would react, no idea what I would do, where I would go if he decided he didn't want us. If he'd even let me leave. My eyes had lowered as I'd prepared myself to speak. But I looked at him now, searching his face for any hint of reaction.

There was none.

He got up, stepped into his pants, and pulled a T-shirt over his head.

"I'll find a doctor," he said.

And without looking back at me, he left.

20

Vasile

AFTER I DRESSED, I moved through the motions of the day, meeting with Priest, other clans, settling disputes within Clan Petran, but it was almost as if I was in a dream.

I was preoccupied, to say the least, with Fawn's announcement.

Pregnant.

I didn't know how I felt about it. At some point, I knew I would have a child. It was my duty to my clan, one I would fulfill. But this, a child created out of desire not duty... I wasn't yet sure what to think.

But no matter what, I would have to keep them safe, keep the ugly taint of my world from touching them, something I knew from hard experience was a near impossibility. No matter what I tried, how I tried to protect them, Fawn, the baby, would now always be at risk. I could build a fortress, have a thousand men, and if I slipped just once, they would be taken from me.

"What's the bad news?" Sorin asked, plopping a glass down in front of me before sitting across from me.

Still grappling with my thoughts, I hadn't yet gone home, wasn't sure what I would say to her.

"She might be pregnant," I said on a heavy exhale.

Sorin smiled bright and stood and rushed over, almost tackling me with his hug.

"I didn't think you had it in you," he said, slapping my back heartily. "I hope he takes after the good-looking side of the family. My side." He laughed and clapped my shoulder again.

Then, after he looked at me for a moment, he sobered.

"Shouldn't we be doing shots? Celebrating? You're going to have a son, but you look like you just got the worst news ever," he said.

"This is very serious business, Sorin," I said.

"Isn't this the very definition of *not* business?"

"Everything is business, and everyone around us is tainted by it," I said.

Sorin waved a dismissive hand. "Vasile, you always find a way to make everything suck. You should be happy, thinking about your son and not that other shit. Business takes care of itself."

"No it doesn't. And it's that kind of attitude that holds you back from becoming the leader, the man you should be."

He frowned, piercing me with his stare, but then he said, "Don't make this about me, Vasile. Lecturing me isn't going to change the fact that you're too fucking stupid and stubborn to celebrate a blessing. Something we don't get all that often."

I stared at him and shook my head. "Don't you understand the risk? They're targets now."

"Yeah, so? She was a target before," he said.

"'Yeah, so.' I should fucking punch you, *prostu pulii*."

"Not if I punch you first. Father, Grandfather, his father before him, they all had kids. This shit works out."

"How many uncles have we lost?" I said.

Sorin shrugged. "Across the generations. Twenty. Maybe more. But so what? The Feds could bust in here right now, send us to prison for the rest of our lives. Deport us. Some other clan could try to take us out and take control of the organization. A fucking tornado could rip this building to shreds and us with it. So what, because bad things can happen, we run and hide?

"Get your head out of your ass, Vasile, and try to be happy for once. The shit's gonna touch us, and all of us aren't going to make it out, but right now, you should be with your woman. Celebrating. Asshole," he said with a shake of his head.

I looked at my brother with new eyes, wondering when he had started to grow up.

"Perhaps," I said grudgingly.

He smiled again, reminding me of the pesky, cocky kid that had been like my shadow. "Perhaps?" he said. "You know I'm right, brother, but I won't make you admit it. I'm going to celebrate," he said, rubbing his hands together gleefully.

I put a hand on his arm. "Sorin, keep this quiet, okay?"

"Yeah, yeah," he said, and then he headed off.

After he left, I thought about what he'd said. Maybe he was onto something. And then again, maybe he wasn't. But in this thing he spoke the truth. This was a time for celebration, and I should spend it with my woman.

When I arrived home, I found her sleeping. I crawled into bed beside her, wrapped my arms around her waist, put my hands on her belly, and fell asleep with images of my new family filling my mind.

21

Fawn

"YOU'RE DRIVING TODAY?" I asked.

"Yes. I want to be alone," Vasile said.

The churn in my gut sped to hurricane speed, and I worried I might pass out from the wave of dizziness that hit me.

I'd been nauseous for a couple of weeks, but this bout was not brought on by what had been confirmed as a pregnancy, at least in my mind.

No. This was dread pure and simple. Disbelief that he was making me do this.

"Fawn, we must go. We don't want to keep the doctor waiting," Vasile said.

He looked at me patiently but expectantly, hand on the door handle, and though my mind screamed at me to run, I complied. He got in after me, and then drove off, guiding the car with sure, efficient movements. He was intense as always, but he didn't seem especially bothered. He glanced over at me quickly before turning his eyes back to the road.

"It's early, but I wanted to see the doctor before he opened for the day. We're going out of town because I want this to stay secret. But it will be quick. Don't worry."

I gripped the door handle, surprised when I didn't toss whatever meager contents remained in my stomach.

Left hand on the steering wheel, he reached over and patted my knee. "You'll be fine."

"I don't want to do this," I said, hating the weakness in my voice, terrified of how he might react.

"Why not? Are you afraid of doctors? My grandmother, she was too."

I was almost sick with confusion. This was as close to idle chatter as Vasile had ever gotten, and it had me even more off balance.

"I'm sorry, but this isn't easy for me. I know we didn't plan it, but I want to keep it."

There. I'd said it, and I'd deal with the consequences.

"Of course we'll keep it. What else would we do...?" He trailed off and gripped the wheel tighter and looked at me, pure malice in his eyes.

Then he pulled off the road and parked, expression calm, but the rage that poured off him was palpable.

"Where do you think we're going, Fawn?" he asked. The low, firm tenor of his voice, the precision with which he spoke only heightened my fear.

"To the doctor. To..."

"To what?" he asked flatly.

"To get rid of it," I said, my voice trembling with the fear that had begun to spring up.

He gripped the wheel tighter and muttered a low oath.

"You think I'm going to take you to kill my baby?"

When he asked like that, used that voice, those words, I saw the stupidity of it. He would kill everything, anyone, before he would harm his own, and I wanted to curse myself for even entertaining the idea he would make me get rid of it.

"I'm sorry," I said, sounding frail, pathetic. "I just thought..."

"That I was a monster. That I would force you to..."

He trailed off, and I worried he might rip the wheel right off the car, he gripped it so tight.

"I am, you know?"

"What?"

"A monster. A very bad man. Maybe that's why you can't believe me. Don't trust me."

His words pierced right to my very core, and shame overtook the fear.

"It's just that you didn't seem happy," I said.

"I wasn't," he confessed.

"So you see—"

"But then I thought about it, thought about my son, a tiny little baby with your eyes. I was happier than I've ever been."

He looked at me then and I saw the truth of it in his eyes, felt the fear and shame displaced by love, hope for our new family.

As he turned back to the road, he put his hand on my knee again. I reached out and entwined my fingers with his.

"It might be a girl," I said.

He just squeezed my hand and lifted the corner of his mouth in a smile.

22

Vasile

Five Months Later

"YOU'RE STILL HERE?" SHE said when she woke.

"Yes," I replied, choosing not to say I'd found it harder and harder to be away from her, that seeing her first thing, her body soft and ripe with my child, her eyes bright with affection was the fuel I needed to get through the hours that would pass before I saw her again.

She kissed me, her touch still sweet, almost shy, but her comfort with me real. Her eyes darkened with something but she smiled it away.

"I guess I should get up. I'm seeing Esther today."

"Wait," I said, and she paused and looked at me. "What were you just thinking?"

Her smiled dropped an increment, but I didn't press, just waited.

"I just... That day. Why did you...?"

"Take you?" I asked.

She nodded.

I'd considered that question a thousand times and had finally settled on an answer. "You reminded me of someone. My turn," I said.

She nodded again.

"How did you find him?"

She chuckled grimly. "You mean how was I stupid enough to get captured by him? To allow myself to be broken by him?"

"Fawn—"

She turned her eyes toward me. "What? It wasn't my fault? I couldn't have known?"

I went silent, but then grabbed her hand and squeezed it, urging her to go on.

"Vanity," she finally said.

I squinted in question, but she wasn't looking at me, didn't see me. Was lost in those horrible memories of the past.

"I graduated high school and I needed a job, decided I was going to be a real professional. I ended up at a temp agency, and they sent me to David's office. It was his father's back then, but I didn't know that, didn't know anything. Was just a stupid kid pretending to be an adult."

She looked at me then, but I still didn't think she saw me. "Don't know how I caught his attention, but one day he stopped in front of my desk, said I had a pleasing telephone voice." She laughed derisively. "Pleasing telephone voice," she spat. "Something as stupid as that, and I felt like the queen of the world. Important. Special." Her voice went quiet then, and I saw the anguish in her expression.

"He was so sweet, so nice. And then one day he wasn't," she said on a deep sigh.

"He hit you," I said, knowing full well the answer but needing to hear her say it.

"Hit me. Kicked me. Choked me. Whatever caught his fancy at any given moment," she said casually.

I paused, rage making me dizzy, the desire for retribution making it almost impossible for me to stay still, sadness at what she had lost, happiness at being with her now, making me stay. When I thought I could speak again, I said, "Did you try to leave him?"

She looked at me then, face twisted in disgust. At me or herself, I couldn't tell.

"I didn't try. I did," she said. "Waited until he left one day and then snuck out. Went to Esther's house."

She looked at me again then, reading the question on my face. "So what happened?" she said.

I nodded.

"What always happened. I was stupid, let myself get comfortable. Let myself believe that he'd let me go. I was there over a month, had almost convinced myself I was safe. And then one day..."

She trailed off, eyes turning down, face dropping. "Someone slipped an envelope under the door. There were pictures inside, pictures of Esther, her grandmother, her little brother."

"David," I said.

"Or someone who worked for him. Didn't matter. I got the message loud and clear. I left that very moment, didn't even say good-bye," she said. "And he was waiting on me, opened the door before I rang the bell."

Her voice was a near whisper, and I clenched my fists to try to help bite back the emotion. Whatever she was going to say would not be pretty.

"I was terrified, but he was on his best behavior. Hugged me, told me how much he'd missed me. Had me make his favorite dinner. Steak and corn on the cob. And he sat, drank his wine, and talked to me about everything that had happened at work while I was gone."

Her eyes were flat now, far too reminiscent of the way they'd been the very first time I'd seen her.

"He finished his last bite of steak, took the last swallow of wine, and then he grabbed the bottle..."

She went silent, lost in thought, but she didn't have to continue.

"I thought that I wouldn't make it, prayed that I wouldn't, but I got better."

"And?" I said.

"He got worse. I couldn't go outside, couldn't

pick my clothes, my food, anything. It was awful, worse than awful, and I spent every moment of every day trying to do whatever I could to keep him happy, trying not to set him off. That was entirely a futile task, one that drove me to the brink of insanity. Beyond."

The dread that had brushed at my mind now gripped it full force. "What happened, Fawn?"

She pulled her sleeve up, turned her arm toward me. I'd seen the scars, but hadn't asked where they had come from, probably unwilling to consider the answer.

"They're fading now; you almost can't see this one, but it feels so big to me," she said, stroking a finger across the thin line nestled in the crook of her elbow.

"He tried to kill you?" I said, unable to keep the shock out of my voice.

"Every day. But this," she said, stroking the mark, "this is from me. I decided one day that he would never let me go, and I couldn't take another day, another second, so I took one of his razors. Did one, then the other, and then I lay there and prayed for death. And again my prayers went unanswered."

He'd robbed her of her will to live, had broken her precious spirit to the point that death was better than life. Rage, anger, and sadness again overtook me. After a moment, I spoke, "He saved you."

She laughed, the sound caustic, bitter. "Saved me? No. But he nursed me back to health, smothered me with attention and affection, said he couldn't wait until I was strong again.

"And when I was, he beat me. Said he was the one who decided whether I lived or died."

She stopped then, lowered her head, the weight of the shame pressing down her shoulders, her face.

I squeezed her hand tighter, reached up with the other to cup her cheek. "Not him, no one, will ever lay a hand on you again, Fawn. Not ever," I said.

I held her eyes with mine, hating the sadness I saw there, the disbelief, but I wouldn't look away until I knew she believed me.

I couldn't say when the change happened, but she reached up and grasped my face as I did hers, and then she lay a soft kiss against my lips. I stayed still, let her kiss me as she wanted, ignoring the need that being near her always stirred.

She deepened the kiss and ran her hands across my chest, touching me with passion, acceptance, that made me sigh. Then she broke the kiss and stared into my eyes, her own hooded with desire. I almost protested when she turned, but held my tongue and watched as she lay on her side and then pressed her back to me, her ass curving against my cock. I curled behind her, rested my hands on the expanse of her stomach and then moved down to delve between her legs, found the wetness there.

I needed to be close to her, could sense she felt the same, so I guided my cock into her and stroked slow and gentle as I kissed her, let my hands trace her body until she reached a gentle climax that drew my own.

Later, I held her close, listening to each of her breaths and swore I would never let darkness touch her again.

✷

"LET ME MAKE YOU feel good, Daddy."

The cheap whore shook her huge tits in what David supposed was an attempt to entice him. His dick didn't even twitch. Hadn't in what felt like forever, not since he'd lost her.

Not since she'd been taken by that son of a bitch.

The whore brazenly ran a hand across his thigh and waggled her eyebrows. In the club, she'd reminded him of Fawn. But under the brighter lights of his private rooms, the resemblance disappeared. She was curvaceous, though not as much as Fawn. Her face was attractive and objectively, David could acknowledge her features had a refinement Fawn's didn't. But her eyes killed the illusion completely. Where Fawn's had been soft, almost innocent, the whore's eyes were hard, gleamed with calculation.

The sharp slap rang out, and it was only then that David realized he had reached out.

The whore's eyes widened, then went flat with resignation. She'd probably expected it, and the look in her eyes enraged him. There'd been times when he'd had to hurt Fawn to teach her something, but every time she had been surprised, and though he knew she'd tried to hide it, every time there had been pain.

He missed that. Missed her.

He hit the whore again, this time with a closed fist, the dull sound of bone against bone making his dick jerk with the first signs of life for a long while.

She grabbed her cheek, and David slapped the other.

The whore retreated into herself, seeming to shrink before David's eyes. That got another twitch and David smiled.

The whore was no Fawn, but she'd do well enough until he got Fawn back.

He punched her in the stomach.

23

Fawn

I JOLTED AWAKE AT the sound of a slamming door and sat up abruptly, looking wildly around the room, noticed immediately Vasile wasn't here. I glanced at the clock and noted the hour. Two thirty. Not so late that it gave me pause, because there was no rhyme or reason to his comings and goings, but when he'd left earlier, he said he'd be back soon and it had been several hours.

I'd wanted to stay awake and see him when he returned, knew that even though he'd never said so, he liked to see me at the end of a long day, maybe even looked forward to it. I was happy to oblige him. As I stood, I stretched, the baby's little kick making me smile.

"You miss your daddy too?" I said, a hand on my stomach.

I headed down the stairs toward the kitchen, but as I approached, the hairs on the back of my neck rose, and an uneasy feeling rushed through me. It was quiet, too quiet, and even though the men Vasile had insisted be at the house at all times made an effort to not disturb me, this felt different. Eerie.

Cautiously, I went into the kitchen, noticed the French doors were open, and when I looked through them, I gasped.

Oleg, wearing his tank top even though there was a chill in the air, lay on the kitchen floor in front of the open doors, an ever-expanding pool of dark blood growing around him.

My mind wanted to reject what I saw, but the blood, Oleg's still form, the furious pounding of my heart made that impossible, and the fear I thought I'd finally left behind came flooding back. I turned, my mind racing as I moved, planning to grab my car keys and leave.

I made it two steps and then stopped short.

"I told you it was time to come home," David said.

My throat went dry, and my racing thoughts slowed, stuck on one. David was here, in our home, and there was no one to protect me.

Strangely, though I was afraid, terrified really, I managed to beat that back, stayed calm. David was always unpredictable, volatile, but my only hope was keeping him as calm as I could, and I couldn't do that if I let my fear show through. "You need to leave, David. You don't want—"

"You're done telling me what to do, bitch."

In an instant, his cool facade faded, and the monster from the nightmares that still sometimes haunted me stood before me. I wanted to be strong, but I couldn't help the tremor of fear that racked over me.

"David, it's over. Please leave," I said, surprised that I managed to keep my voice moderately even, and that I didn't look away from him.

He narrowed his eyes, the expression so familiar, yet one that felt like I had seen it in another lifetime. Still, I knew what that expression meant, what came after it. I couldn't let that happen, wouldn't risk myself or my baby. I took two steps back.

"What did I tell you?" he said, stalking toward me slowly. "What!"

I said nothing, which enraged him even further.

"It's been too long. Playing house with that motherfucker made you forget. But I'm going to remind you. It's over when I say it's over. You belong to me. And only me."

Never, though I wouldn't tell him that. I continued to back up, moving deeper into the kitchen as he walked forward. The French doors were open and maybe if I got out there, I could call for help.

I continued to move back slowly, trying to put as much distance between us as I could. And then suddenly, I turned, running as hard and fast as my body would take me.

The door was getting closer, and though I moved awkwardly, my socked feet slipping on the marble floor, the awkward angle of my belly hampering me, I still ran.

"No you don't," David said.

He was muscular and while I knew those muscles came from chemicals and a rigid weightlifting routine, I also knew he had no stamina. Rage must have fueled him though, for before I could reach the door, he grabbed me, one arm snaked tight around my shoulders and one around my waist. He spread his palm over my belly, and of all the things he'd done to me, as revolting as I found his touch, nothing was worse than this, his hand on my stomach, touching my baby, our baby, as if she was just another of his possessions.

"This might be mine, you know," he said, breath fanning over my ear, his voice cold, menacing.

My mind rejected the words, the very idea and in a display of carelessness, I freed my tongue. "She's not," I said. "Nothing here belongs to you, not anymore."

He tightened his hand until I felt the first bite of pain, but I didn't let it show, wouldn't give him the satisfaction.

"You better hope it is," he said. "'Cause if it's not, you'll never see it again. And neither will he."

Rage and dread warred for dominance, and rage won.

"He's going to kill you for this," I said, not trying to contain my scorn. "But if you leave now, he might not make you suffer."

At one point in my life it might've scared me, knowing Vasile, the man I loved so deeply was capable of cruelty, of murder. But not now. David had gone too far, would finally get what he deserved, and the only thing that saddened me was I hadn't had the courage to do it myself.

"You forgot who the fuck you're dealing with. I have friends, very powerful ones. I take care of people's money, and nobody, not even that son of a bitch can fuck with people's money without consequences."

David sounded certain, which terrified me. He'd never dare cross Vasile, or anyone else for that matter, without support. And then it hit me. This was really happening. He was here, and he was going to take me and my baby. I couldn't let that happen, would die before I did.

As I stood, I imagined what he'd do, what punishments he'd have in store for me. And even if Vasile managed to find me one day, it would be too late because David would surely break me or kill me trying to.

I moved before I had time to think, grabbed the fancy blender Sorin had bought, saying I needed more fruits and vegetables in my diet. It was glass, and it was heavy, so heavy, it didn't even shatter when I slammed it against David's head. After I hit him, his grip slacked enough for me to run again.

"You fuckin' bitch!" David screamed.

I heard him behind me, and then I felt him, his heavy weight pressing me down. I reached out wildly, searching for anything to break my fall. But there was nothing. I put my arm under my belly, felt the impact as searing pain erupted in my abdomen.

And then the world went black.

24

Vasile

PRIEST AND I LEFT Vargas's house and headed toward my car, the peaceful night a sharp contrast to my swirling anger.

"What the fuck was that, Priest?" I said.

"I don't know," he replied.

He looked as annoyed as I did. Neither of us appreciated being called away for bullshit.

"I know we're supposed to have open communication, but I won't be jumping for every little thing. Vargas has his territory and if he can't manage it, he'll lose it. My clan won't be bothered with his internal problems," I said, frustrated I'd been called away from Fawn over nothing.

"I agree. But that was..." Priest said.

"Fucking bullshit. Calling me from my

home for—"

Ice froze my heart in my chest.

"Go!" I yelled at the driver.

Vasile

"FAWN! OLEG!" I YELLED, but there was no response, and I pulled my gun as I proceeded, the house that Fawn had turned into a home suddenly forbidding, menacing.

Something was wrong; I knew that immediately, but I prayed to a god that I didn't even believe in that she was okay.

"Fawn!"

I went to the den, saw the place where Fawn usually lay on the couch, but there was no sign of her.

"Come quickly!" Priest yelled.

I ran toward the sound of his voice, the urgency in it filling me with even more dread. Priest was never urgent; this could not be good. I rushed into the kitchen and my hands dropped to my sides, fingers loosening as the gun I held fell to the floor with a clatter.

My gaze was glued to Fawn's prone form, and I barely heard Priest's words. I saw a dead Oleg and the open door, but that was background noise because I couldn't tear my eyes away from Fawn, or the blood that pooled around her, couldn't believe what I was seeing.

She lay flat on her stomach, not moving. But I didn't go to her, couldn't. She was so still. I shuddered. She looked—

"She's not dead," Priest said, and that confirmation broke the cement that had held me in place.

I didn't carry a cell phone, and an ambulance would probably take its sweet time getting to us anyway. I had no other choice, so I rolled her, feeling some small measure of relief when she moaned. But it was only the confirmation that she was alive, because everything else about her looked otherwise, like the vivid life that had animated her had been ripped away, and it left me breathless, on the verge of panic with worry.

Her skin was bluish, ashen, but that couldn't hide the huge bruise on her cheek or her blackened eyes. And worse yet, her legs were covered with blood, blood that still dripped from her fast enough that it left a trail behind her as I ran to the car.

Priest hopped into the front seat, and I lay Fawn across the back and sat next to her. He slammed on the gas before I'd even closed the door. She looked so peaceful, and though I knew she breathed, I didn't know for how long.

"Not yet, Fawn," I said on a raw whisper, voice wavering with the desperate fear that threatened to overtake me, only held back by the fact that as I held her hand, some warmth returned to it. "Just hold on. Both of you."

Six minutes passed between the time I first

saw her and the time I ran into the emergency room, but it was long enough for me to determine what would happen if I lost her. Whoever had done this, anyone who'd helped was dead. But if she didn't make it, I would seek my vengeance and then join her in death. There could be no life for me without her.

"She needs help," I bellowed, ignoring the shocked faces of patients and staff.

The once bustling room went silent, and then sprung to life, doctors and nurses swarming around me.

"Lay her here!" someone yelled.

I did, and then she was whisked away. I rushed to follow, but a tight grip on my arm stopped me.

"You can't do anything in there."

It was Priest, and I turned to look at him, noting he seemed to have recovered from his earlier urgency.

"Find them," I said.

He nodded and was gone in an instant, leaving me alone, the fate of the only woman I'd ever loved, the baby I had just begun to accept, hanging in the balance.

Vasile

"HEY," I SAID WHEN she finally opened her eyes.

It'd been hours since they had let me back

into the hospital room where they'd put her, and I hadn't left her side.

She looked around the small room, cheery curtains on the windows and neutral paint on the walls only managing to make the place feel even more depressing. And then she laid a hand on her stomach and then pulled it away.

"The baby…"

"Is in the nursery. A girl just like you said," I whispered as I smoothed her hair. I'd been convinced I was having a son, but that didn't matter now. My heart gave a funny little thud. Fawn and I had a precious baby girl.

"Have you seen her?" Fawn asked, the skin around her eyes crinkling with a slight smile.

"I wanted to wait for you," I replied, barely able to get out the words.

"I'm ready," she said.

She wasn't. I could see the pain on her face, the confusion. Also the determination.

"And so you shall," I said.

I left the room and found a doctor.

"Take us to the nursery," I ordered.

The man's eyes widened, and then he nodded.

He looked down at the chart he held in his hand. "Pregnant woman with bleeding?" he asked, looking down at my bloody clothes.

"Yes. Take us to the nursery."

"I will, but I was coming to see you. We should talk before you go. Is your wife awake?"

"Tell me," I said, the dread I felt earlier almost minimal in the face of the anticipation of what the doctor planned to say.

His eyes clouded, and his face settled in a grim line.

"I'm sorry. Another week, ten days, then maybe she would be stronger... But her lungs just aren't developed. We're going to do everything we can to save her, but I'm going to be honest with you, this is a grave situation. You and your wife should prepare as best you can in case..."

I'd been waiting on those words, had expected the worst, but hearing them crushed me in a way I hadn't thought possible. I hadn't completely wrapped my head around the idea of a baby, and now she fought for her life. She had been mine to protect, and now there was nothing I could do for her but be there and wait. For the first time in as long as I could remember, probably since I was a very young boy, tears welled in my eyes. I bit them back, begging them not to fall, and when I finally had regained control of myself, I looked at the doctor.

"Take us to the nursery," I said.

The doctor nodded.

25

Vasile

"I THINK SHE SMILED," Fawn said.

Her voice was watery with tears, but I could hear the joy underneath.

It was afternoon now, the first hours of my daughter's life. But instead of celebration, we were together, huddled behind closed hospital blinds. The NICU was mercifully empty, and that was where we were staying, Fawn holding the tiny baby as much as she could. It had been torture of the most profound kind to watch Fawn hold our baby and then give her to doctors and nurses who poked and prodded, all in attempts to make sure my daughter lived. I wished I could take every jab of a needle, every tube that was threaded into her, take every little cry that she exhaled, her tiny chest near caving before it expanded again.

But I couldn't, could do nothing but stand there, weak, impotent, as helpless as my child. And my failure didn't stop there.

It was shameful, weak, but I'd barely been able to look at my daughter, couldn't bring my-self to touch her. I'd created her, and I'd almost destroyed her before she'd had a chance to live.

Fawn would never forgive me for this.

I would never forgive myself.

"Vasile," Fawn said softly, her voice pulling me out of my thoughts.

I walked over, kneeled beside her.

"We should name her." Fawn smiled, the moment of happiness crushed under the weight of the despair that flickered across her face a second later. "Maria. I always liked that name."

"It's a good name," I said, barely able to push the words out around the lump that clogged my throat.

"Hold her," Fawn said, lifting her arms.

I paused, my mind racing with the thought that maybe me not touching her would protect her, keep her safe as I had been unable to do. I looked to Fawn, and she stared back, eyes bright with the sheen of tears that had not yet spilled.

I had to do this.

So I reached for her, my heart giving a kick when she stirred in my arms.

"*Salut*, Maria Petran."

I lifted my arms and pressed a kiss against

her tiny head.

"*Draga mea,*" I whispered.

She stirred again, then went still.

And so I sat, Fawn beside me, my daughter in my arms, tears running down my face.

26

Fawn

"THEY SAID I CAN go home tomorrow," I said.

"Good," he replied.

"Maria has to stay."

He nodded. "I'll have someone bring you back whenever you wish," he said.

And then, as he had during the entire four days I had been here, he turned back to the window and looked out, standing still, silent sentinel. Everything hurt, my head where I'd hit it, my breasts, heavy and full with milk my daughter could only barely drink. And so did my heart.

I'd loved Maria from the instant I'd learned of her existence, had let myself make plans, dreamed of the life I would give her. And she was fighting for her life because of me, because

I hadn't been strong enough to protect her.

I hadn't been strong enough to keep Vasile either.

He'd only left my side long enough to change out of his bloody clothes, and I don't think he ate or slept. But he hadn't looked at me, barely spoke to me. The only moment he betrayed an emotion was in the NICU with Maria, but even that was clouded with guilt, anger, heartbreak, probably all three.

"The police want to interview me," I said.

"I know."

"Should I talk to them? What should I tell them?"

He looked at me then, green eyes shards of ice. "Tell them whatever you want. I won't interfere." Then he turned away, his rejection another dagger in my already bleeding heart.

I didn't know what that meant and started to ask him, but with another glance at him, so stiff and detached, the words died in my throat.

There was no reaching him, not by me, not anymore. Before I could stop it, a tear rolled down my cheek.

Vasile

SHE WAS SILENT, BUT I could feel her heartbreak. And it wasn't just the tears that rolled down her face that told me. I felt her watching me, furtive like she'd been before, unsure, tentative. I didn't blame her, knew I deserved worse, but I was thankful. She didn't want to see me, could probably not bear spending time in my presence, but I couldn't leave her, and she, for reasons I didn't understand, was kind enough to let me stay.

"I must call and make arrangements," I said abruptly, and then I left the room without looking at her.

It was a bitch move, weak, and my father would have slapped me if he were alive, but I couldn't take it. She was trying so hard, offering me her pity and not her scorn, but I couldn't accept it.

I'd done this to her, done this to my daughter, and every second that she'd lain in that bed, pretending that she wasn't in pain, physical and emotional, had been excruciating. No less than I deserved, but Fawn didn't, and yet there she was bearing the burden of my mistakes, her arms empty because of me.

Sorin milled in the hallway as he had for days, my usually exuberant brother calm, quiet, Natasha at his side, her own spirit unusually dampened.

"How is she?" he asked.

"She's going home tomorrow," I said. "Have a car sent."

He nodded and then asked, "The baby?" Sorin's voice hitched around the word.

"Fighting, but they don't know if she'll make it."

"She will," Sorin said with certainty, something I wished I shared.

"Natasha," I said and she stood.

"Go to the house, have the blood cleaned and have all of the..." I trailed off and then took a deep breath and continued. "Have the nursery emptied."

"Why?" she asked.

"If..." I trailed off, not able to continue.

"But shouldn't Fawn—"

"Go," I said.

Natasha's mouth dropped open at the harshness in my tone, but she nodded and then headed down the long, overly bright hallway.

I stood with Sorin, listening to the others in the hall, the sound of joyous laughter, the cry of babies.

But there was no laughter for us, only worry about whether she would live.

I looked at Sorin, whose eyes glittered hard and certain.

No, Fawn and I didn't have laughter.

But there would be vengeance.

27

Fawn

"MISS MICHELLE?"

I looked up at the sound of my name and the light knock, as did Vasile, who stood when he saw a man I didn't recognize come in. He flashed a badge.

"Detective Murphy, metro homicide. Is now a good time to talk?"

"Homicide?" Vasile said.

The detective glanced at Maria, and almost involuntarily, I pulled her closer. "As we understand it, Miss Michelle's baby is not out of the woods yet," he said.

His words were almost matter-of-fact, but I saw through them, saw he was attempting to get to Vasile, who mostly managed to avoid the bait. "Maria Petran is doing fine. Is there something we can help you with?"

As Vasile spoke, he'd moved to stand between me and Detective Murphy and now, both men eyed each other, seemingly uncaring I was there.

"I'd like to speak to Miss Michelle. Alone."

"That's not necessary," I said. "I can speak in front of him."

"For purposes of this investigation, it's best you don't, ma'am."

I looked at Vasile, who looked at Murphy.

"Okay," I said.

Then I stood and handed Maria to him. He took her and without a word, or even a glance at me, turned and began to pace the small nursery as he always did when he held her. Whether his lack of communication was because he trusted me or didn't care what I might say, I was unsure, but I wanted to get this over with. I followed Detective Murphy down the hall and we went into a small office, probably for nurses or something, and I sat in the seat he gestured toward. There was another man in the room, but he didn't introduce himself, and I didn't care to ask.

"You reside with Mr. Petran, correct?"

I nodded.

"Speak. We're recording this," the unnamed man said.

"Yes," I said, happy my voice didn't waver.

"And have you witnessed any criminal activity inside his home?"

"No," I said.

"Miss Michelle, I know you're afraid. You have every right to be, but we can protect you. He's a violent, dangerous man, almost killed you and your child in the process. We can't fix that, can't make sure that your baby girl lives and isn't...damaged. But we can make him pay for what he did to you, what he's done to others."

I'd known it would come to this, but I'd expected it after hours of priming, so I had to give Murphy credit for not wasting my time.

"I'm not sure what you think is happening, but Vasile had nothing to do with what happened to Maria."

Murphy's face folded into the most scornful scowl. "Do you believe that, or are you just covering for him? You baby almost died, ma'am. Still might, and you're covering for that..."

I felt my own anger rise, but I bit it back. I'd gone to the police once, and they'd taken me right back to David. And now they wanted me to betray Vasile.

Wouldn't ever happen.

"It's time to feed my baby. Is there anything else?" I asked.

28

Fawn

"I GET ALL OF this personal service?" I said, smiling at Sorin after Vasile helped me into the car.

He smiled back, then looked quizzically at the huge pillow I had pressed against my stomach.

"For the bumps in the road," I said.

He nodded. "You won't feel a thing." Then his smile dampened. "Fawn, I'm sorry she's not coming with us," he said.

"Thank you, Sorin. For everything," I replied. He'd been there every day and had taken to Maria right off. It impressed me, showed a side of him I'd never seen.

"Drive," Vasile said, effectively ending the conversation.

Sorin turned and then drove away from the

hospital, slow and sedate. The car had a funereal atmosphere, the wrongness of leaving the hospital without the baby dampening everyone's spirits, and even Sorin, who was usually so hotheaded, was subdued.

But true to his word, he got me home with minimal pain.

"I'm impressed," I said. "I'm seeing a different side of you."

"I can be different. With family," he said, the significance of his words not lost on me.

Vasile, who'd rounded the car and opened the door, touched my shoulder. I went to stand, but he put his arms around me gingerly and then scooped me out of the car.

"Comfortable?" he asked.

I nodded, and then he set off, moving quickly but somehow managing not to jostle me.

He moved up the stairs with the same speed and tenderness and then lay me on our bed, carefully arranging me.

"I will bring your medicine later. Rest," he said.

Then he leaned forward and placed a chaste kiss on my forehead and was gone in a blink.

Those few minutes in his arms had been the most comforted I felt since that awful night, but now, back in the house I hadn't known if I'd ever be able to face, in a home that was more empty than it ever had been, I was alone, cold.

And I knew that he blamed me for what had happened, knew that Vasile was lost to me.

Vasile

A FEW HOURS AFTER I'd brought Fawn home, I followed the sound of Sorin's voice to the front door, saw him standing with his body blocking the portal, his face set in a scowl.

"Why are you here?"

"I came to see Fawn," Esther said.

"She's not feeling well."

"She asked me to come."

I hadn't known that, but I had expected her sooner or later.

"Sorin, let her pass," I called.

He stood aside reluctantly, scowling down at Esther. But she paid him no attention and instead turned her eyes on me. I'd seen her many times since that first one, and this was the only occasion when I hadn't been able to read her emotions completely. She was veiled, hidden, but I thought I saw pity in her eyes.

And blame.

The blame I could take. The pity I wouldn't abide.

"Why are you here?" I asked, not bothering to modulate my tone.

"She asked me to bring this."

Esther's voice was bland, devoid of her natural attitude. The surest sign that something, something else, was wrong.

"And who let you up here?" Sorin asked,

standing close enough to touch her, his stance intimidating.

She didn't seem bothered, and instead casually tossed over her shoulder, "I can be persuasive."

She tightened her grip on the black bag that she held, and I focused on it, suddenly suspicious.

"What is that, Esther?"

I stepped toward her as I spoke, and she looked up at me, eyes still hooded, her grip on the bag tightening.

"It's personal," she said.

Sorin snatched the bag out of her hand and opened it.

"What the fuck is this?" he asked.

He looked into the bag and then handed it to me. I stared down and then I opened it and glanced inside. I closed it immediately and handed it back to her. She had thinned her full lips into a harsh line, her expression grim.

"What's that for?" I asked, hating the raw note in my voice.

Esther sighed. "She has to do something with her milk when she's not at the hospital."

The words were another stab in the chest, a reminder of how wrong things were, of how my baby wasn't home with us where she should be. I watched as she brushed past Sorin and walked up the stairs.

When she was gone, I gestured toward the den and he followed me.

"Those fuckers are gonna get what's coming

to them," Sorin said, pacing around the den with the pent-up energy he'd thankfully managed to suppress while with Fawn.

I stared at him, and he stopped, looked back at me. "What are you waiting for? It's already been days. You have to hit and now!"

"What have you and Priest found?" I asked, surprised I managed to say anything at all. When I wasn't thinking about Maria, hoping with a fervor that almost scared me she would live, vengeance was at the fore of my thoughts. It wouldn't take away Maria's pain, Fawn's, even my own, but it would set some things right, and I nearly salivated at the thought of getting it.

"Ashmore."

Just the sound of his name sent me into a near blinding rage.

"I'd assumed as much," I finally said. "He had help." I knew that had to be true as well because Ashmore wouldn't have risked it alone, but I wondered who else I would soon make suffer.

"Yes he did. Seems your little meeting with Vargas was a distraction."

"Vargas helped him?" I asked.

It didn't matter, wouldn't change either of their fates, but I wondered why. What made Vargas agree to forfeit his life for Ashmore's gain?

"He owed Ashmore's old man a favor. It has been collected."

"Were any of the other clans involved? Anyone else?"

Sorin shook his head.

"You sure?"

"I'm sure. So what are we going to do?"

I looked my brother in the eye.

"Kill them all."

29

Fawn

AFTER ESTHER LEFT, I managed to fall into an uneasy sleep, probably aided by the pain medication. I awoke to find Vasile standing beside the bed looking down at me, his face that distant, unreadable mask that I'd seen far too much of, his body shrouded in the semidarkness of the bedroom. I felt the attraction I always did when I looked at him, but it soon dissipated in the face of overwhelming sadness. We'd gotten closer. He'd opened up to me, and now that connection had been severed, probably wouldn't ever come back.

I reached for him, but he covered my hand with his and gently pushed it back down on the bed.

"Easy. Don't push."

His hand lingered on mine, and I wanted to grab it, hold it to me, but when I reached for him again, he pulled away.

"Vasile..."

He stared down at me, face now determined. I knew what would come next.

"You have to go?"

He nodded.

"Do you know when you'll be back?" I asked, hoping he'd say it was soon, praying he would in fact come back.

"No," he said.

"But when you come back, it will be done," I said. I'd guessed as much, had seen how not responding was eating at him and could only hope that once it was done, we could start to build the little family that I had only dreamed of, me, him, and Maria, together, happy.

"It will be done."

He stood silent then as if waiting for me to say something. But there was nothing I could say. I could tell him that nothing would come from more killing, say what was done was done, but that was bullshit. He never, ever, involved me in his business, but he seemed to treat his men fairly. But this, an attack on his home, on his child, would be punished severely, fatally and I was happy about it.

I felt so weak, so useless, especially since there was no way I could help him. But I could give him my support. Before he could react, I grabbed his huge hand, kissed his rough fingers.

Then I stared up at him.

"Do it. And then come back to me."

A short nod was his only response.

Vasile

"HE IS IN HIS home?" I asked.

"Yes, he's being acquired now," Priest said.

"Good. He'll be my second stop."

I drove toward Vargas's, an eerie feeling of déjà vu at the back of my mind. It had been less than a week since I had last done this and in that time, my entire world had burned down.

This wouldn't fix it, wouldn't fix anything. But it was something I had to do. When I'd told Fawn, I hadn't been sure how she'd react, and I still couldn't tell how she had. She'd gone mysterious, unreadable as she'd been that first day. Did she think me a monster?

Probably.

The things I would do tonight would not dissuade her.

I parked in Vargas's driveway and then got out, unconcerned about being seen.

"This is where I leave you. I hope you find peace," Priest said.

"I didn't come here for peace," I replied.

I entered the huge house, heartbeat accelerating at the first whiff of the air.

Then I followed the muffled whimpers up the

stairs into the opulent bedroom. My gaze landed on Sorin, who stood with the others, face flat, eyes hooded. I nodded quickly and then turned my attention to the rest of the room.

The walls were covered with reminders of his Incan heritage. He'd have a connection to his homeland in these last moments, which was more than he deserved.

I strolled to the middle of the room where Vargas lay duct taped to the bed, spread eagle. His mouth was gagged, and he moved his head furiously, his screams muffled.

"Hello, Vargas." I smiled. "Is there something you'd like to say?"

Adrenaline raced through me, setting my heart to pound but with excitement not fear, and a part of me hoped Vargas would lie, would give me a chance to stretch this out.

He nodded frantically, and I walked over and peeled the tape off his mouth slowly, and as always, he disappointed.

"I'm sorry. I tried to talk him out of it, but I owed his family. The debt had to be paid. You understand. I had no choice."

"Of course you did," I said casually, managing to keep a hold on the rage threatening to boil over and force me to end this far earlier than I intended.

"I didn't, Petran," he sobbed, shaking his head violently.

"You did. You chose poorly," I said.

I extended my arm, and Sorin handed me the small container. I walked a circle, pouring the accelerant on the mattress, and then dousing Vargas.

He closed his eyes and then began to whimper, the sound faint yet ferocious.

"Do you know what that is?" I asked.

He mumbled in Spanish and didn't respond.

"I asked a question, Vargas," I said.

He shook his head.

"It's turpentine. An amazing substance. It'll suffocate you eventually, scar your lungs until they stop working. But it burns slow, eats away at you layer by layer. And you'll be awake for it all. I'll make sure of that."

"My wife! My kids! Where are they?"

Instead of responding, I tossed a match onto the bed and watched as the sheets and then Vargas were eaten by flames.

Vasile

"YOU PROBABLY SHOULD KILL them too," Sorin said. "The wife and kids."

"Probably," I said flatly, "but I think she's smart enough to disappear. I don't want any more innocents to suffer unless they have to, and I don't think she cared enough to give her life for Vargas. Besides," I said wearily, "everyone is watching, and while I will get my vengeance, I think the others might appreciate some restraint when it comes to the women and children."

"I think so too," he reluctantly agreed.

And then I went quiet, my mind full to overflowing with thoughts and emotions I could barely contain.

My hands tingled with the excitement of what I was about to do. It should have disgusted me, and maybe somewhere deep inside it did. But it also filled me with the first hint of satisfaction I'd felt since I'd found Fawn on that floor, my baby's life seeping out of her. So it may have been wrong, but I wouldn't pretend my vengeance wasn't something I looked forward to with racing anticipation. Something that I would savor, relish, something that would, to whatever small degree, make at least one small thing in this world right.

Sorin, seeming to sense my mood, stayed quiet during the drive.

When I parked, I turned to him. "You and the others stay here," I said.

He looked me up and down, but I couldn't tell what he thought and didn't care. My mind was already inside the abandoned warehouse, my body explosive with anticipation.

"I'll be here whenever you're ready," Sorin said.

I got out of the car.

30

Vasile

"LET ME UP, MOTHERFUCKERS!" David yelled, defiant till the end.

Which was fine by me. He could yell all he wanted. It wouldn't change anything.

I entered the building, breathing deeply, trying to calm my racing heart. I halfway wondered if when I saw him, I'd be so overcome, I wouldn't be able to stop myself from killing him instantly. I really, really hoped that wouldn't happen.

I had plans.

Still, my hands shook with the energy that flowed through me, and with every step, my heart pounded a little harder.

And then I saw him, and everything stopped.

He hadn't been touched, just as I had ordered,

still somehow managing to look as if he owned the world. Even the fact he was bound to a chair with no hope of escape didn't seem to bother him.

"So that's how it is, huh? You're supposed to be this big boss motherfucker. Your clan and your honor and all that bullshit, and you're gonna do it like this? Kill a man without giving him a chance to fight back?" he spat.

"A chance to fight back like Fawn had? Like my baby had?" I yelled, my voice sounding monstrous even to my own ears.

He went quiet and something in his face changed. Then he said, "Look, Petran, I didn't mean for that to happen. But we got a good thing here. You have to think about the other clans, the Peruvians, the Sicilians, everybody! I handle all their money. You're gonna have a lot to explain if you do this."

Almost dizzy with anticipation of what I was about to do, anger at what he'd done, I stepped closer as he spoke, and when I stuck my hand in my pocket, he stopped, face going alert with curiosity and wariness. I pulled the small needle-nose pliers from my pocket, not trying to hide them.

He swallowed nervously, and his eyes went wide.

"I'll leave you alone. I swear, you will never see me again."

"The first true thing you've said," I said.

And then I stepped closer, the pliers tight in my grip.

Vasile

"I'M SORRY," DAVID SAID.

He was fading, and so was I. These last hours had been taxing for both of us.

He turned the eye that he could still open toward me.

"You stole her from me," he said on a thick, slurred voice. "She was mine. And then she wasn't, because you took her!"

I ignored him and instead ripped the remnants of his bloody shirt off his body, exposing his arm. My gaze zeroed in on the fat, juicy vein that sat in the crook of his elbow.

"That mark on her arm, the one that you put there. She touches it sometimes. I don't even think she realizes she's doing it, but I see it. She touches it and then gets this look in her eye."

"She did that herself! I fucking saved her..." He cut off on a deep cough, the blood he brought up dribbling out of his mouth and onto his chest. I ignored him though, instead focused on that vein, thought I could hear the blood rushing through it, felt my lungs squeeze tight with the excitement of the thought of opening it.

"You remember what you told her? That she could only die when you said so?"

He gurgled and said something indecipherable.

"Answer me!" I yelled.

"Yes," he pushed out through swollen lips.

"That wasn't true. You took from us, took from her, but she's still here. Will be long after you're not even a memory."

I wrapped the pliers, now slick with David's blood and my sweat around that vein. Then I clipped, watched as the blood gushed from the wound, fast at first and then slower, and then even slower until it was just a trickle.

He went limp and I waited. Watched the blood drip, drip, drip out of him.

A long time later, I left.

Vasile

"YOU DRIVE," I SAID to Sorin.

I was so exhausted I could barely move, but I felt something that approached peace. I'd never heal, would never forget, but he no longer breathed. And if I'd never given Fawn anything but suffering, at least I could say I'd given her that. Small, but maybe it would help me make amends for so profoundly failing her, failing both of them.

The ride home was a blur as was the walk up the stairs. I stripped and went straight to the second bathroom, not wanting to bring my filth to her. And then, more tired than I could ever recall being, I stumbled into the bedroom.

She jolted and then turned to me. I stumbled and kneeled next to the bed, my head next to her. She reached out to me, and I clasped her hand in mine, feeling that rightness, relief, that I always did with her. It was different now, but it was there nonetheless, and I prayed that at least some of it would survive.

And then I slept.

31

Fawn

Three Months Later

I TOOK A DEEP breath and then knocked on the door. He'd told me I didn't have to do that, but what he said and how I felt were seldom the same thing, not when his words welcomed me with open arms but his voice, his body, his ice-cold eyes told me to stay away.

He opened the door and stood in the entryway, looking down at me with a frown and question on his face. He seemed the same physically, imposing form, cold expression, but he was burdened now, changed, and even though I couldn't imagine all the things he'd seen and done in his life, I could see that he was different, weighed upon.

I planned to do my part to lift at least some of that burden.

"I'm going to Esther's," I said.

"One of the men will take you. Stay as long as you want."

He turned, but stopped when I spoke. "No, Vasile. I'm going and I'm staying." He looked at me, seemed to notice for the first time the bag that I held in my hand. He focused on it and I saw a fleeting flash of regret across his face. But then his expression closed, and he shut down completely.

"It's probably for the best. I'll have someone watch the house."

And then he again turned to walk away, but I stood rooted in my spot, frozen. I knew I was doing him a favor by removing myself, but to hear him so casual, almost relieved, broke what little was left of my heart.

My vision watered, and the room went blurry.

"You want this. Why are you crying?" he asked, sounding as if he was inquiring about the weather or some other mundane concern.

"Why wouldn't I cry? There's so much to cry about," I said.

"Like what?" he said, voice flat.

Anger, burst through the pain, sharp and stinging.

"We almost lost her, Vasile! Our daughter, Maria. You remember her, don't you? She's in the hospital, but she's coming here soon, back to what was supposed to be our home," I said, voice hitching.

He visited her every day, but when we were inside these walls, he acted like I, like she didn't exist. Had even emptied her nursery. "Just in case," he'd said, like not having her stuff here meant I wouldn't get attached, that he wouldn't get attached. He'd shoved her into a box, tried to keep himself distant so it wouldn't hurt as much if she didn't make it. Seemed he was trying to do the same to me.

"Don't be stupid," he said, voice harsh, icy eyes filled with pain.

"Too late."

He had come back to me, and through watery eyes I could see the serious expression on his face, the anger that was the first sign of life that I had seen in him for months. As then I was grateful for even that, welcomed any sign that the person who had captured my heart might still, somewhere, exist.

"You know I don't like that, Fawn," he said, voice edging dangerously.

"Why does it matter? I was stupid, stupid to think I had a chance," I said.

"You have a chance. And he won't ever hurt you again."

"He doesn't have to hurt me—he's done his worst. He almost took my daughter from me. He did take you away from me. He won."

I met his eyes and was shocked to see surprise there.

"Me?"

"He did, didn't he? You don't look at me. You don't talk to me. You pretend like I'm not even here. So I may as well not be."

His face dropped, something almost like confusion crossing his features, so unlike him.

"I..." He reached up to hold my face in his hands, his eyes on mine. "I can't... When I look at you, I see how much I failed you, her, can't imagine why you'd spend a moment with me. How you could ever forgive me if we lost her." He swallowed, his fingers tightening on my face. "Lost Maria."

His eyes dampened, and I saw the agony in them. I grabbed his wrists, squeezed, hoped that the touch told him that I loved him, that I didn't blame him. That she was going to be all right. I believed it with all my heart.

"It's not your fault," I said, voice hard.

"It is. You, her, you were mine to protect. And I failed. And I'll never forgive myself for that." His face and eyes had gone rigid as he spoke, and I felt him slipping away.

"Not even if it's the only way?" I asked.

"The only way for what?"

"The only way for us to move forward. If you don't, he will have won. I don't want him to win. And I don't want to lose you," I said.

"You'll never lose me. You have my heart forever, Fawn," he said.

He stroked his thumb along my jaw and then leaned forward and pressed his lips against mine. It had been so long since he'd touched me like that, and the feel of his lips against mine, gentle yet firm, reminded me of all those times before, of the times I hoped we'd have again.

He deepened the kiss, thrusting his tongue into my mouth as he held my face tighter. And then he dropped his arms and let his hands roam my body, gripping at my breasts, across my back, down to cup my ass. When he roughly pushed my pants and panties down my legs and delved his hand between my thighs, I broke the kiss and cried out.

I locked my eyes on his as he ran his fingers across my slit, coaxing moisture from me. His ice-green eyes went darker and all of the emotion that I'd missed, the feeling I thought had left filled them. I saw the pain, the turmoil, the desire, the hope.

Without speaking he half dragged me to the couch and in three deft motions, lowered his pants, settled me over him, and pushed me down on his cock. His thickness spread me, the stinging pleasure making my lungs freeze. With one hand on either of my hips, he kept his eyes on mine and moved me over him, pushing me down as he thrust up, the rhythm jerky, erratic, almost frantic.

I understood well, and with each thrust, I could feel the walls falling, the connection that had pulled me to him, made me stay when it had seemed insane to do so come back full force.

And I could see the love in his eyes. Under the pain, the sadness, it shone bright and true.

I kissed him them, swallowed his each harshly exhaled breath as he pounded into me, took me to heights that only he ever could.

My climax came fast and hard, a lightning strike that had me crying out.

"I love you, Vasile," I said on a low moan.

He went even harder inside me and then stilled, grasping my face in his hands, his eyes on mine.

"*Te iubesc*, Fawn," he said as he emptied his seed inside me.

Later, after he'd carried me up the stairs and to the bed, we lay, limbs entwined, his hard body behind me, cocooning me with warmth and love.

ᴍ

Fawn

One Month Later

"THAT'S EVERYTHING?" I ASKED.

"Yes. We got the nursery done yesterday and finished bringing everything else in. And Maria Petran is officially home and asleep in her own bed for the very first time."

Vasile smiled bright, full as I'd ever seen him at that last word. We'd had setbacks, but our baby was home, healthy, and we were together.

I watched him as he peeled his clothes from his body, climbed into our bed, and held me close. We lay there entwined, quiet and somehow I knew that like me, he was thinking about how we'd started, how far we'd come. Where we might go in the future.

"So you're going to keep me?" I finally asked, voice quiet in the dark of the room.

"Always," he replied.

THE END

About Kaye

Kaye writes hot, gritty, suspenseful romance featuring alpha males and the women they love. You can find her at her website:

www.kayebluewriter.com

Read on for an excerpt from *Fall*, the second book in the Romanian Mob Chronicles...

1

Esther

"DICK," I WHISPERED UNDER my breath, but still loud enough for Sorin to hear me. I was standing right next to him after all.

"Bitch," he replied, not bothering with the whisper.

"Smile!" Fawn said, the bubbly excitement in her voice more suited for a party than the battle that was about to break out in front of her.

I shook my head. Smile? Here I was standing in Vasile Petran's foyer like he wasn't a secretive, dangerous Romanian mobster and Fawn wanted me to smile?

Of course, Vasile wouldn't harm me, and in fact went out of his way to humor me since I was his woman's best friend and his daughter's godmother. So as crazy as it was, Vasile wasn't the problem.

His brother Sorin on the other hand...

I felt my face squelching into a scowl at the very thought of my newest and most despised nemesis.

A squirming baby Maria brought me back to the present, and I looked up at my best friend, smile plastered on her face and her eyes screaming at me to smile with her or else. But I ignored Fawn's demand, ignored the silent admonishment to behave. Ignored everything except *him*.

Well, him and the near-dizzying rage that pounded at the base of my skull.

How could something so simple—a picture with a baby for God's sake!—end up with me in a homicidal rage and him looking as if he felt much the same way? I shouldn't have been surprised, though. Sorin Petran had a way of making me want to murder someone, and today was no exception.

"I said smile. And no more name-calling. Either of you," Fawn repeated, this time dropping her overly bright voice into one of threatening.

I turned my gaze to Sorin, waited for him to react.

And waited more, but he kept those laser-blue eyes on me, normally fullish lips—not that I'd noticed—set in a grim line, chiseled face stark with his flat expression. His body was at ease, the huge, loping muscles seemingly relaxed, but I wasn't fooled. His right hand was clenched tight, and if he clamped his jaws together any harder, he'd break a tooth.

Bastard.

He had no right to be pissed. He was the one who treated me like a nuisance, an *outsider*, like I didn't belong in Fawn's life or Maria's, while I went out of my way to keep the peace. Or rather, didn't go out of my way to *not* keep the peace, something I easily could have done. And my thanks for it was being ignored at best, or facing his completely unrestrained scorn at worse.

My gaze caught on the flex of his jaw as he gnashed his teeth, which only emphasized his strong jaw, the rough-looking stubble that covered his cheek, the kind that would add just the right amount of friction as he—

I dropped my gaze quickly, trying to redirect the train of my thoughts, but instead landed on the strong column of his neck. Looking at the wide breadth of his shoulders didn't help either, and by the time I'd settled on the middle of his chest, my pulse was pounding, and not with the anger that still roiled inside me.

Double bastard.

It was so fucking unfair. My nemesis, the only storm cloud in my and Fawn's newly rekindled friendship, and he had to be the hottest, sexiest, most delectable man I'd seen in ages, hot enough to make me question my vow to only chase nice, decent guys.

Like I said, it was so unfair. Something

that was reinforced when I finally looked at his face again, saw those shocking blue eyes, the angry little flair of his nostril. After the fresh stab of anger, a thought struck. If he was going to be pissed, I might as well give him a reason.

Quick as lightning, I closed the space between us and pressed my lips against his, my eyes open as I watched his anger shift to shock and then back to anger before making its way back to shock.

"Fawn said smile, Sorin," I said in a candy-sweet voice as I stepped back, my own smile lifting into overdrive when he narrowed those lethal eyes at me.

Then I turned to Fawn, shifting Maria so she was between Sorin and me, knowing I had a goofy expression tacked on my face and not caring one bit.

I would have had to look away eventually, would have had to show that his intensity could get to me, but this, this was perfect. However temporarily, I had gotten the upper hand and managed to wipe that smug smirk off his face for the first time.

"I guess this will do," Fawn said as she snapped the picture and then looked down at the camera. "Now give me my baby."

Without a word, Sorin lifted Maria from my grasp into his huge hands and arms, the tattoos that covered both making quite a contrast when he held the small bundle wrapped in pretty pink against his chest. He whispered something to her that I didn't understand and then hummed quietly, voice soothing, safe, so not like the Sorin he showed me.

But Maria had that effect on people, and if nothing else, I couldn't doubt the depth of love we all felt for her.

"No one can ever see that picture, Fawn. Erase it," he said as he handed the baby to her. Then he quickly kissed the top of Maria's head and left, all without acknowledging my presence.

Fawn eyed me, but didn't speak as she walked toward the living room, me in tow. She fussed with Maria and got her settled in her bassinet before she turned to me.

"I want to hold her," I said with a pout, ignoring Fawn's pointed expression.

"No. Between Vasile, Sorin, and you, she gets held plenty."

She kept her eyes on me, waiting. Her expression was neutral, but I could tell she was expecting an explanation. But what could I say?

I deployed the most convenient weapon I had on hand to win a victory in the not so cold war that rages between me and your man's brother. That would have sounded crazy, even for me, so I chose distraction.

"What did the doctor say?" I asked as I moved closer.

My plan had worked. She brightened, her face taking on that reflective expression she always got when she talked about Maria. "He said she's looking good. She gained three pounds, and he says she is catching up nicely after her setbacks."

"That's good!"

"Yeah with her being a preemie and then those issues she had with swallowing, it's all going great. But he said we have to watch her for," she swallowed, "potential developmental issues, but she's doing good," Fawn said.

My heart squeezed as I watched her rub Maria's soft little arm, saw the love and concern in her expression. After Fawn's attack and Maria's early birth, the baby's survival had been far from certain. But she was tough like her mother, and I knew she'd be fine.

Fawn smiled down at her daughter and then looked at me, eyes sharp, expectant.

I waited, now convinced my distraction had only been short-lived, and wondered if maybe, for the first time, Fawn would cut me slack and buy into my attempt to avoid the subject.

No such luck.

"I'm gonna sit on you if you keep looking at me like that, shorty," I said after a moment. It was a common threat, one I'd used since we were kids when Fawn was a short little thing to my tall and heavy. That much hadn't changed, nor had the fact that Fawn always ignored me.

"What was that about, Esther?"

"What?" I said as I plopped on the couch and faced Fawn when she followed.

"Fine. Play that game. Why do you insist on antagonizing my brother-in-law?"

"Brother-in-law?" I said eyes widening. "Have you been holding out on me?"

I exclaimed. I'd seen the love and affection between her and Vasile, knew that he cherished her and Maria, and though there had been a few bumps in the road, I'd never doubted that they would be together, and marriage felt like the logical next step. I'd even considered the possibility that they'd done it in secret.

Her expression deflated, and her shoulders slumped, and I wanted to punch myself in the face. Though Fawn had never said so, I knew this was a thorny subject, Vasile's position and her past making theirs more complicated than boy meets girl. And of course I'd gone and put my big foot in my bigger mouth.

"Sorry, Fawn," I said. "Maria can beat me up if you want."

She gave a slightly pained smile and then sat next to me and sighed. "No, don't worry about it. I haven't even brought it up to him. I just thought..."

As she trailed off, she looked toward the closed door, no doubt thinking of Vasile. "It's complicated, and I know he loves me, so maybe in time..."

"If you want it, you should tell him," I said.

She scoffed. "You've met him, right?"

I laughed. "Yeah, once or twice. Besides, you probably shouldn't take relationship advice from me. I'm better at keeping jobs than I am at keeping men. And I suck at keeping jobs."

Fawn smiled, then sighed. "I don't know

why I even care. I mean, he loves me, and I know we'll be together."

"But there's something to having it official. You're not wrong for wanting that," I said.

"Maybe, maybe not. But we're not talking about me." She turned sharp eyes on me again. "You were saying?"

"I wasn't saying anything."

"Esther..."

"It's not my fault! Sorin's a douche. He fucking stares at me like I'm scum or like he wants to shove my dead body that he deaded into a barrel filled with lye."

She laughed out loud. "Esther, that's not true."

"You're right. He probably has people who do that for him," I said.

"You're ridiculous, Esther. Sorin can be... intense. But that doesn't explain why you act like that."

Her brows dropped and she tilted her head and then a slow smile spread across her face. "Esther Jordan, you want to fuck him."

"You kiss your baby with that mouth?" I said, trying for all the world to sound shocked at the very implication, like the very idea of running my hands over Sorin's inked skin while he scraped that ever-present beard against my most sensitive places had never occurred to me.

And it hadn't, not *that* often, anyway. How could it have? I didn't even like him.

Fawn just nodded. "Mmm-hmm. I do kiss

my baby with this mouth. And it makes sense now. All that clucking and those insults and generally churlish behavior. You're trying to cover up."

"I do *not* cluck. And your baby brain is showing, Fawn," I said. My voice was strong, but the way I withered under her glare gave me away. Still...

"Come on. I'm not in elementary school anymore. I'm not going to be mean to a boy because I like him. Be for real."

I scoffed and waved a hand dismissively, turning my head at the same time. I kept an eye on Fawn, though, waiting to see if she'd bought it.

No dice.

"Look," I said, scrambling to come up with a reasonable story, one that didn't involve me confessing that a certain Sorin had played prominently in my dreams for months now. "He's...attractive." Nuclear hot, but that was semantics. "But he's also a psycho and a giant tool, always scowling at me, asking why I'm around. It's annoying as hell."

She gave a sympathetic nod. "They can be uncomfortable around newcomers."

She didn't expand on that point, but she didn't need too. The Petrans were well known enough that their ties to organized crime were an open secret, one that left me uneasy, more than uneasy. But in one of the few moments of reticence I'd ever had, I didn't ask for details and Fawn didn't provide them. I didn't care who Vasile was, what he'd done. He'd brought my friend back to me, and that was all that mattered.

"It's cool, I get it, but the dude needs to take it down a few notches and relax."

Her lifted eyebrow stood in place of the unspoken, *And you need to do the same.*

"You have to admit, though," I said, "the look on his face when I kissed him was priceless."

"Yes it was," she said on a laugh, "and I'm not deleting that picture. Maria can look at it when she gets older and try to figure out why her uncle and TiTi looked like they want to murder each other. Or, you know, someone else."

"Whatever," I said, looking away again and feeling something far too close to embarrassment for my liking. Stupid Sorin.

"Don't you have to work today?"

I smiled, looked back at her. "No."

"Esther, did you quit?" she said, narrowing her eyes at me again.

I glanced away, that embarrassment increasing. "No, I got fired. But it's not my fault this time, Fawn! What happened was..."

Sorin

"DOES SHE EVER GO home?" I asked, looking at the closed door when I heard the muffled sound of women's laughter.

"Is that why you're in here instead of with Maria? Hiding from a woman, Sorin?" Vasile asked.

"Trying to respect my brother's home, something that"—I stopped short at his frown—"*she* makes difficult."

It was too hard to even choke out her name. Even thinking it, thinking of her, sent a rush of annoyance through me.

"Esther's a good friend, kind, loyal. You saw how she fought for Fawn," he said.

"I saw her butting in where she had no place."

Vasile shrugged casually. "Maybe, but not many would stick their neck out for a friend like she did, something I thought you'd appreciate."

I looked at him, noting the difference as I considered my response. He was happier than I'd ever seen him, smiled more, seemed freer. But there was also a weight that hadn't been there before. Both of us had accepted out eventual fates, knew that jail or death were the most likely places we'd end up. But he carried the burden of seeing after his woman and child now, and though they weren't mine, I knew that it was heavy because I carried it too, knew that I would do anything to protect both of them.

I slammed out of my seat, frustrated as always seemed to be the case when Esther was even mentioned.

"It's good that she's loyal, but she's also... unruly. And an outsider."

"Since when has a little unruliness bothered you, brother?" he asked.

"Are you fucking with me?" I said, spinning to look at him and the smile that he didn't even try to hide.

"Maybe a little," he replied, laughing then, the expression on his face reminding me of a time so very long ago when he'd been free, had been just Vasile, my big brother, and not Vasile Petran, leader of Clan Petran, weighted by all that came with it.

I shook my head. "She tests me."

"That's not a bad thing. It'll keep you sharp. Besides, you know what I think?"

I suspected what he thought and had no interest in hearing him share it, so I said nothing, which didn't discourage my suddenly talkative brother.

"Everyone falls at your feet because of the name, that pretty-boy face of yours. Not Esther, though. And you don't like it."

I grunted my disagreement. My issues with Esther had nothing to with how little my charm seemed to affect her.

"No, what I don't like is how she's always around. She's not family. Clan," I said.

"She's Fawn's family, and will be treated as such."

"Yeah, yeah," I said, drifting back to the chair I'd recently vacated, trying to push thoughts of Esther and how much she pissed me off aside.

"You're going to Familie tonight?" Vasile asked.

"Yeah, but I'm dropping by Petey's first."

"Good. There's been talk about Clan Constantin. Christoph is in poor health."

"Has he named a successor?"

Vasile shook his head. "Not yet, and time's ticking."

"Two sons and Anton and he still doesn't know who'll take over. What a fucking mess. This could get ugly, especially if a more ambitious soldier sees an opening."

"It'll be up to you to contain the fallout," Vasile said.

"Yeah. I'll let you know what I hear," I said as I stood.

I left and headed toward the front door. I stopped and almost turned around when the sound of Esther's voice drifted down the hall toward me, the sound sparking an awareness that wasn't quite annoyance, one that made me want to escape if only to avoid figuring out exactly what it was.

But after a brief moment, I continued. I was Sorin Petran, brother of the leader of Clan Petran, a powerful and feared man. No one, not even Esther Jordan, would make me cower.

"So I have the interview at the hardware store tomorrow," Esther said as I turned the corner.

I stopped, looked at her, seeing that for once she wasn't wearing a scowl on her face as she stared down at Fawn who held Maria. She actually looked...pleasant, almost friendly. Nothing would ever make her exactly pretty, but the soft smile on her face almost did the trick. I took the moment to watch unobserved.

She was very tall, closer to my height than Fawn's, solidly built with sturdy legs, thick waist, broad shoulders. There was nothing dainty about her, in body or mind, but there was a certain appeal in her. One wouldn't have to worry about being delicate, handling her like she was fragile. Not that anyone could get close, not with her slashing tongue and fiery eyes.

"You got fired again," I said before I could stop myself.

She pressed her lips together, her smile dropping in an instant. Then she turned slightly, looked me from head to toe before turning back to Fawn.

"So wish me good luck," she said as she leaned in to half hug Fawn around Maria.

She was ignoring me, dismissing me, and I thinned my lips into a grim line and pierced her with a stare. And she noticed. Tried to pretend she didn't, but I saw the momentary pause, saw her gaze as she shifted it to me but then looked away quickly.

I relaxed my face and nodded, some of the tension leaving. I was not one to be dismissed, and Esther now knew it.

"I'm not worried. I know you'll get the job," Fawn said.

Esther huffed. "Yeah, I just have to keep it,"

she said, her voice light with humor. "Catch you later."

"Wait. It's dark out. Someone will drive you home," Fawn said.

"I'm cool. Bye-bye," she said, and with one last look over her shoulder, she walked out.

"You leaving, Sorin?" Fawn asked.

I nodded, and she met my eyes, put her free hand on my arm. "Take care."

"Always," I said and then left.

I thought about them, Fawn, Maria, even Esther, as I drove away, how normal they were, how I'd never had people like them in my life before. People who weren't of my world.

And soon, I didn't think at all.

It was time for work.

Other Works

Romanian Mob Chronicles

Keep
Fall

Men Who Thrill

The Enforcer
The Assassin
The Soldier
The Con

Printed in Great Britain
by Amazon

16101972R00130